Across the *Wide River*

Across the *Wide River*

Stephanie Reed

Across the Wide River

Published by Kregel Publications, a division of Kregel, Inc., P.O. Box 2607, Grand Rapids, MI 49501.

Scripture quotations marked KJV are from the King James Version of the Holy Bible.

Cover design: John M. Lucas

Library of Congress Cataloging-in-Publication Data
Reed, Stephanie.
Across the wide river: a novel /by Stephanie Reed.
p. cm.
1. Underground railroad—Juvenile fiction. [1. Underground railroad—Fiction. 2. Slavery—Fiction. 3. Christian life—Fiction. 4. Ohio—History—1787–1865—Fiction.]
I. Title.
PZ7.R2529Ac 2004
[Fic]—dc22 2004013952

ISBN 0-8254-3576-5

Printed in the United States of America

05 06 07 08 / 5 4 3 2

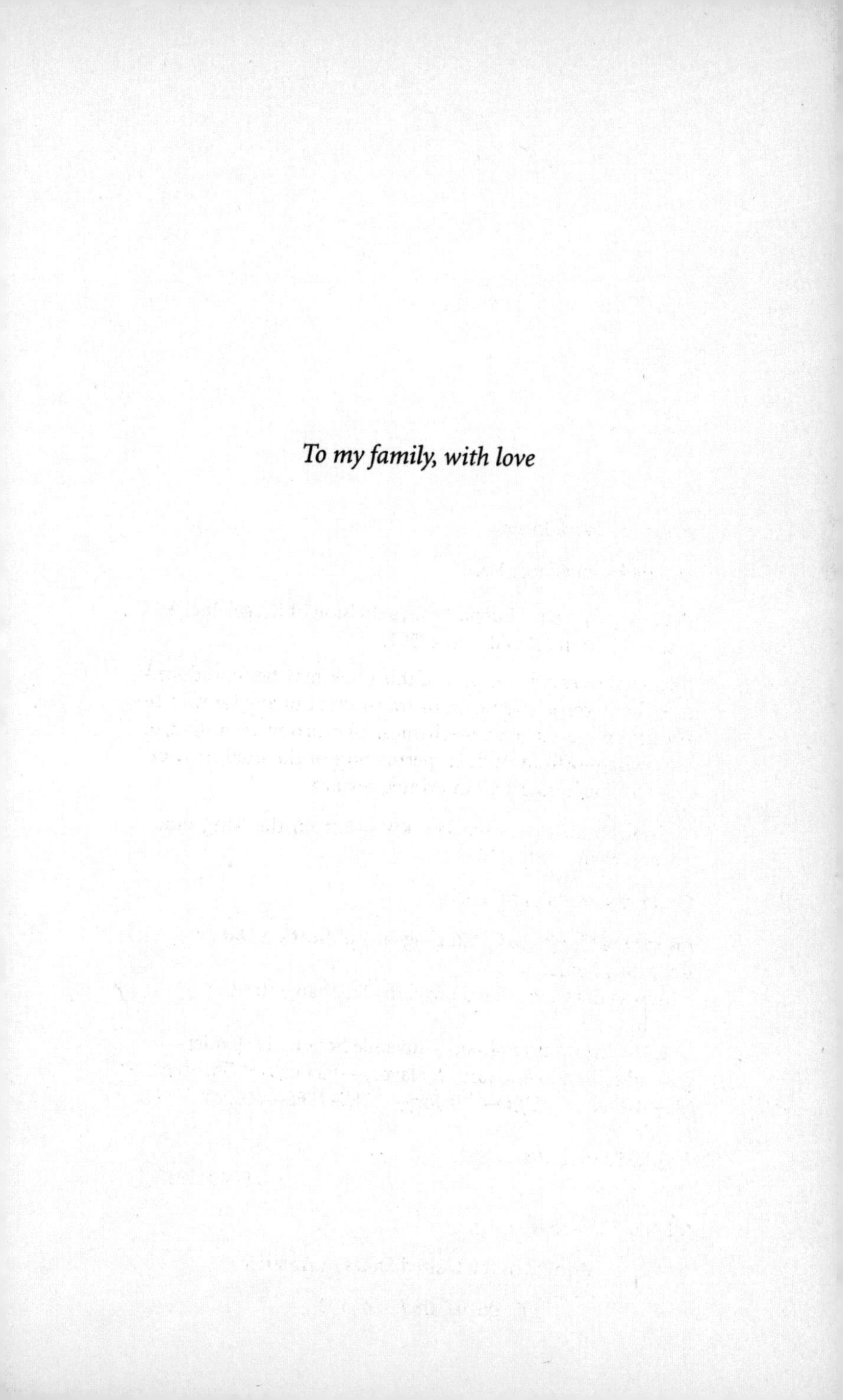

To my family, with love

Acknowledgments

For their help, the author is grateful to

- ALISON GIBSON, Director, Union Township Public Library, Ripley, Ohio
- OHIO HISTORICAL CENTER, Archives/Library staff
- RUSSELL WILHOIT, Local historian, Decatur County (Indiana) Historical Society
- BECKY F. AND DAVE L., editors extraordinaire
- DENNIS, WENDY, JANYRE, STEVE, and the rest at KREGEL PUBLICATIONS
- ANN HAGEDORN, author of *Beyond the River,* et al.
- TREVA PICKENPAUGH, Branch Head, Huber Heights Public Library
- THE REVEREND PETER MARSHALL, author of *The Light and the Glory,* et al.
- JIM POWERS, retired history teacher, Rankin descendant, and friend
- JANE T. F., Rankin descendant, and her cousin, JEAN TIGER S., who passed away of emphysema in 2000
- ROSS AND CAROLINE G., Rankin descendant, his wife, and their son, LARRY G., who passed away in 2000 of Alpha One, a hereditary condition (1-800-4-ALPHA-1)
- BARBARA C., Rankin descendant and my cherished friend, who passed away of breast cancer in 2002

Author's Note

THOUGH THIS BOOK IS A work of fiction, the Rankin family was real. In fact, I once "found" a descendant of David Rankin as we walked together down a narrow path to visit the Rankin House in Ripley. Many other Rankin descendants provided me with information and even shared copies of family photos. I spent, not months, but years doing library research—I wanted to know the whole story of the Rankins!

Even though Father and Lowry each wrote autobiographies and Johnny wrote several accounts of slave escapes, no one recorded the whole story. Armed with straight facts about the Rankins and the times they lived in, an Ohio-Kentucky background, and some imagination, I have not written the history of the Rankins, but the *story* of the Rankins.

At www.ohiomemory.org, you may search for "Rankin" and find the Ripley Anti-Slavery Society charter, where the names of Lowry and Ibby Rankin, and many other Ripley residents, are entered. There is also a photograph of John and Jean Rankin, Lowry's parents.

The slave owners, traders, and hunters found in this book were real people, but their names have been changed. Sherwood was real, although I am not sure of his name. Old Sorrell was real, too; Lowry wrote a touching tribute to him in his autobiography.

Even though I had to imagine some parts of the story, one thing is certain: Lowry Rankin served the Lord Jesus Christ, who is the same yesterday, today, and forever.

Across the Wide River

Chapter 1

THE BOY SPRINTED ALONG the forest's edge in the bright Kentucky sunshine. As he plowed through scarlet maple leaves, they crackled under his shoes and clung to his white knee stockings. The sweet, dusty smell wrinkled his freckled nose. The sleeves of the boy's loose white shirt fluttered as he ran, and he kept one thumb firmly tucked under the waist of his gray breeches.

"Hurry up, Father!" Lowry yelled over his shoulder. Why were adults always slow as molasses? "Sherwood will think we ain't coming for Bible school!"

"Lowry Rankin!" Father sounded far away. "You know better than that."

"Honest, Father, I ain't kiddin'!" He hopped the creek that meandered along a green rise to the distant ridgeline. Suddenly something rolled under his foot and he sat down hard. Rubbing his hip as he retrieved his straw hat, Lowry rustled through the leaves until he uncovered a moldy wooden handle about two feet long. He fingered one gnawed end as Father towered above him with a stern face.

"Son, you're almost nine years old—old enough to know better than that. How many times have I told you that educated people do not say 'ain't'?" Father shifted the Bible he carried to his other hand and pulled Lowry to his feet.

"I ain't sure," Lowry admitted. He hitched up his breeches and tightened the laces at his back. "What's this, Father?"

Lowry heard his father sigh. "Please don't say 'ain't,' Lowry. Try to remember next time."

"Yes, sir. What is this?"

Father's high forehead wrinkled and his eyebrows drew together. "It looks like the stock of a whip."

"For a horse?"

"No, son." Father hesitated so long that Lowry thought he had forgotten what to say. "For slaves. This is hickory. See how thick it is, Lowry. The lash of the whip was fastened here." Father indicated the gnawed end. "It looks as if rats have been at the cowhide. The lash would have been about twelve feet long and as thick as my wrist in the middle."

Lowry crinkled his nose in distaste. "But Father, nobody around here would ever whip a slave. Are you sure that's what it is?"

Father's mouth drooped and his eyes were troubled. "Yes, son. I am absolutely certain. Whippings happen all the time. As a matter of fact, your mother and I have been talking it over, and we have decided—"

"I'll race you, Lowry!" A tremendous shove spread-eagled Lowry into the leaves again.

"—to move to Ohio, where we—"

"Sherwood!" Lowry sputtered, scrambling to his feet. He forgot all about Father, whose words were lost on the wind. Digging in his toes, he ran until the blood pounded in his ears. Maybe today he would beat Sherwood to the log schoolhouse!

Sherwood shot an alarmed glance over his shoulder. Lowry was hot on his heels. Lowry's stomach somersaulted with excitement as he gained on his friend . . . drew even . . . and . . .

Sherwood leapt the stake and rider fence and tripped in a tangle of long arms and legs on the other side. Lowry sprinted through the gate and smacked the schoolhouse door first.

"I win! I win!" His mouth stretched into a smile so wide it made his jaw ache. He threw out his chest and strutted on the porch. He did not see Sherwood wink at Father.

Lowry gathered his breath and pulled the latchstring. The batten door swung open on its wooden hinges. Lowry's shoes clattered on the puncheon floor and he marched triumphantly into the schoolhouse. Father smiled at Sherwood and took the piece of paper the boy was holding out to him—a Bible school pass that his master had signed to say he could listen to Bible teaching if two white people were present. Lowry hung his hat on a peg and blinked while his eyes adjusted from the bright glare of the morning sun to the dim light filtering through the greased-paper window.

"I don't think anyone else is coming, Father. May we start?" The sooner Bible school was over, Lowry reasoned, the sooner he could play with Sherwood. Sherwood nearly always had more chores to do than Lowry did; he guessed it was because his friend was older. Saturdays after Bible school was the only time they could play.

Sherwood sat down next to Lowry on the slab bench, and the boys' shoulders heaved as they grinned at each other. The older boy's lively green eyes and quick smile lit up the room. A sheen of perspiration glistened on his golden skin and a few droplets clung to the tight reddish-brown curls that hung over his eyes. Lowry wiped sweat from his own forehead; there was no need for a fire in the open fireplace today. Father perched on the edge of the schoolmaster's backless chair and opened his heavy Bible.

"Today is the twenty-first day of September, in the year of our Lord 1825. We shall begin with eighth John, verse twelve. 'Then spake Jesus again unto them, saying, I am the light of the world.'"

This text—again! Lowry had heard it countless times. He dutifully trained his eyes on Father, whose words rose unheeded to the rafters as Lowry daydreamed.

Friday, here in school, the schoolmaster had drawn a map of Kentucky on the slate; Lowry could still pick out the dim outline on the wall behind Father. When the schoolmaster had asked Lowry to pick out Carlisle, the town where they lived, Lowry had taken the slate pencil and made a mark smack dab in the middle of the state. Though the master had corrected the placement, Lowry was gratified to see he was not far wrong.

Lowry loved Kentucky. The gentle rolling hills and crumbly shelved ridges hid all manner of wonderful possible pets. He knew it was best to leave the wild creatures alone, but he could not bear to hear the plaintive whimpers of an orphaned baby animal. His parents knew he would not rest until he found the helpless creature and took it under his wing.

He had found a dappled fawn last spring and named it Spot. He and his little sister, Isabella, had cared for the orphan, providing for its every need. If ever a fawn lived a softer life, Lowry never heard tell of it. He did recollect that the fawn grew much faster than he did, and in a very short time, Spot became a handful. One morning, when Lowry had faithfully carried the pail of food out to the pen to feed Spot, the high-spirited fawn crowhopped on its long, matchstick legs, flung out razor-sharp hooves, and stampeded Lowry. He had jumped out of the way faster than a jackrabbit, while Ibby held her sides and squealed with laughter. Spot had charged out of the pen and jaunted off to freedom, but there were many other orphans to be found to take the fawn's place. Lowry was sure that nowhere else on earth was as wonderful as Carlisle, Kentucky.

Father's voice droned in the background as Lowry's thoughts wandered across the countryside. The minutes stretched slower than a dribble of molasses, but Lowry's mind flitted like the swallowtail butterflies he loved to chase.

He had learned the hard way that some animals do not make good pets. On another occasion, while he and Ibby were gathering hickory nuts, Lowry had heard a curious grunting. He had left Ibby for a moment to check the underbrush for helpless orphans, but instead he had found a litter of ugly wild piglets that squealed in terror when he approached. He had just about made up his mind to leave them alone when a roaring wild hog came crashing through the trees, alerted by the distress call of its piglets. Sunlight glinted off the monster's dripping yellow tusks as it charged. Lowry had spun on his heels to run, expecting Ibby to follow, but she had stood motionless, her face white with fear.

"Run, Ibby!" Lowry had screeched. All he'd had time to do was chuck a stone at the hog's face, but it barely fazed the enraged sow. The five-hundred-pound hog, with tusks a foot and a half long, slashed at Ibby, snagging the hem of her linsey-woolsey dress and dragging her backwards over the ground like a rag doll. That was the worst moment, when Lowry knew that Ibby was seconds from death. The hog was about to savage her right before his eyes.

Her screams had pierced his heart. In that moment, he had known he had to *do* something. Clenching his teeth, he had grabbed a stout limb and sped toward his sister. Gripping the branch so hard that his hand throbbed, Lowry had run faster than ever before in his life. Catching up to the hog, he had pounded on its bristled back until the limb cracked in two. With a fierce yell, he shoved the jagged end at the hog's eyes, caught Ibby's arm, and pulled. Her dress ripped as the two of them toppled to the ground. Fortunately, the hog had dodged and retreated. In an instant, Lowry was back on his feet, waving the broken branch menacingly before hurling it at the hog with arms that felt like jelly. He had then crawled back to his sister's side and hugged her as they both sobbed.

For a week, Lowry had been a hero in Carlisle, the envy of his schoolmates. Privately, he thought that if he had to battle a wild hog to be a hero, he would just as soon let somebody else have all the honors.

Lowry had decided there was no room for a wild piglet in his menagerie. But it didn't matter anyway. Mother had recently told him that he must not bring home any more wild pets. He supposed she meant for the time being. Money was tight lately, anyhow, and Father talked a lot with Mother about being "financially embarrassed." But Father was always fussing about something.

Lowry shifted uncomfortably on the hard wooden bench. Why was he suddenly feeling uneasy? He cast about in his mind but could not pinpoint what troubled him. *Wait! It was something Father said just before Sherwood pushed me down in the leaves. Father and Mother had talked over*—Lowry could not be sure, but it seemed as if Father had said something about moving . . . to Ohio!

His stomach fell to his shoes. *Why in the world would Father want to leave Kentucky?* The Rankins had lived here all his life. Well, he had been born in Tennessee, but his parents had moved when he was just a baby. He knew why they had moved that time. It was to get away from slavery. Father hated slavery, just like Grandma Rankin.

When Father talked about Grandma Rankin, it was evident that he loved his mother. From the time Father was small, she had drilled into him that slaves deserved to be free. She would sooner die than force a slave to do her work without pay; she preferred to do it herself. And if a woman as busy as she was finished her work without slaves, she said, then everyone else could do the same.

She spun flax and wool and wove them on the loom into linsey-woolsey cloth to provide clothing for her large family, and the children also helped out with the daily chores. Even when Father was very young, he had swept the house, scoured the floor with sand, and spun flax and wool to help his mother. He frequently reminded Lowry that he had always preferred work to play; in fact, Lowry doubted that Father ever had played. Father's eyes shone as he described how he kept his mother's garden back in Tennessee—he marked straight, orderly rows, weeded (a chore Lowry hated), and tenderly cared for the green seedlings. He had also dressed out the corn and cotton crops, repaired gates, and even fashioned plows in his father's smithy. As he grew up, he had stitched leather harnesses and even cobbled his own wedding shoes. When Lowry thought about Father's boyhood, he felt lazy.

Father had graduated from Washington College in Tennessee, where Lowry's Great-grandpa Doak was the president. Father had married President Doak's granddaughter. That was Mother, and she had named Lowry after her father. Lowry called him Pappaw. Pappaw had convinced Great-grandpa Doak to set his slaves free. Father, raised to hate slavery, had married into another like-minded family. Father could not help but be an ab—abo—something. The word Father always used was difficult, but Lowry knew it meant "no slaves."

The trouble started when Father became a minister. Lowry knew that the church elders had scolded Father when he preached against slavery in his sermons, but he did not really understand why. He did know that Father was not the kind of man who let anyone else tell him what to do. Rather than cease to preach what he believed, he left east Tennessee one fine morning and set out for the free state of Ohio.

Pappaw had given Mother and Father a horse, a two-wheeled carriage, and seventy silver dollars for the journey. Lowry could scarcely imagine so much money! Grandpa Rankin, on the other hand, had not given anything to the travelers. He had begged Father to stay in Tennessee. Father had flatly refused, so Grandpa Rankin did not even come to breakfast on the morning baby Lowry and his parents left Dumplin Creek, Tennessee. As they drove away, though, Grandpa Rankin had rushed out to the stable and mounted his saddle horse. Silently, he'd followed the carriage on horseback while tears coursed down his cheeks.

The heartbroken procession had traveled solemnly for miles until Father finally stopped the carriage. Tenderly, he had reminded Grandpa Rankin that he was a mighty long way from home, almost too far to return safely by nightfall. What words were spoken then, what embraces exchanged, Lowry never knew. Father could not speak of the parting without weeping. He had not seen his parents since that day.

Oh, Lowry could parrot the story of why his family had left east Tennessee, all right, but it was just a tale he had memorized. It did not concern him, except that the Rankins had not made it to Ohio, because the people of Carlisle, Kentucky needed a preacher. At first, Father had refused to settle in another slave state, but the people had insisted, and it had all worked out. The Rankins had learned to live peaceably among the slaveholders.

That thought brought Lowry back to the present. Why would his family move to Ohio now, he wondered, when they were so happy here in Kentucky? He looked up at Father, who was still reading the Bible to Sherwood and him. Father could not have held a Bible school if the slave masters in the neighborhood had not consented, so the masters could not be so bad. Some of them even allowed their slaves to attend church services and be baptized. Lowry's friend Sherwood was a slave, yet he was the happiest boy Lowry knew, always cutting a shine. Sherwood even loved his master, Mr. Roberts.

Mr. Roberts was a kind, rich man who owned a hemp farm. He never raised his voice or his hand to his slaves, and he and Father were good friends. In fact, most of the slave owners in Carlisle respected Father and attended his church, even after the church decided slaveholders could not become official members. One Sunday, a visiting minister had asked Mr. Roberts how he felt about that rule. What Mr. Roberts said had gotten back to Father, who had in turn repeated it to Lowry. "I go quite often to Mr. Rankin's church," Mr. Roberts had answered, "and enjoy his preaching, even if I cannot be a member there. I don't think there is one preacher who does not believe that some time in the future Christianity will destroy human slavery. Well, why not preach it, as Mr. Rankin does? I think he is the most consistent Christian in the state of Kentucky. He has my profound respect, for he does not hesitate to preach and practice what he believes." The words had made Lowry feel proud.

"What's that mean right there, Mr. Rankin?" Lowry sat up straight. Sherwood was asking Father a question in his slow, soft drawl.

"You mean, 'And ye shall know the truth, and the truth shall make you free,' Sherwood?" Father repeated patiently.

"Yes, sir."

Lowry slanted a furtive glance at Sherwood. The older boy was leaning forward and breathing in quick puffs. His eyes shone brighter than a flash of summer lightning. He plainly wanted to know the answer so much that Lowry was ashamed; he wished he had paid more attention to what Father had read.

The next instant, he wished it even more. "Lowry, suppose you explain it to Sherwood," Father prompted. "You have heard this text many times."

Lowry squirmed. Frantically, he wondered why Sherwood was so interested in this particular verse. He was already an honest boy, always truthful. Maybe the truth was what Father was after; maybe he knew that Lowry had not been paying attention. His face grew warm and he hung his head. "I'm sorry, Father. I wasn't minding."

Father sighed. "Well, Lowry, you must do better next time. We must always be ready to give an answer for the hope that is within us." He consulted his pocket watch. "It's powerful warm this afternoon, and past time for you to be back, Sherwood. We'll stop now, but I will be over to visit your master later. I'll explain it to you then."

"Yes, sir." Sherwood's shoulders drooped until Lowry could almost taste his keen disappointment. For the first time, he wondered if Sherwood was as happy as he always seemed.

"You may be excused, Sherwood. I'd like to talk with Lowry privately. Just wait out on the porch. We'll be out directly."

"All righty, Mr. Rankin." Sherwood lifted the latch and pushed the door wide.

Lowry shuffled to the front of the room. "I'm sorry, sir," he began. He half-hoped his apology would forestall a scolding.

"Lowry, I—" Father bit off his words and snapped to attention. The color washed out of his face until he was whiter than a hen's egg. "What was that?"

Then Lowry heard a scream split the air. Was Ibby in trouble again? His skin crawled. He tried to move, to run, but his knees buckled. He opened his mouth to ask Father a question, but Father was gone. Somehow, Lowry followed him out the door.

When he reached the edge of the schoolhouse clearing, Lowry relaxed. A man he did not know stood over some unfortunate animal. He guessed it must be a balky mule, for the man raised a cowhide whip, a whip as thick as Father's wrist in the middle. The leaded tips whistled through the air and the hoarse screams stopped. Then Father sprinted pell-mell and bellowed in his Sunday voice, "Stop! Stop it at once!"

Lowry followed at a distance, curious to see what was going on. He loved all animals, not just wild orphans, and he felt sorry for the poor old mule, but he was surprised at Father's reaction. Then he stiffened. There was no mule. What he saw was a crumpled heap of reddened tow-linen on the ground. He touched it and drew away fingers sticky with blood. Slowly his mind puzzled out the rest of the scene: the long arms and legs, the curly mop of hair, the golden skin that was now paler than a beeswax candle, except where red gashes oozed. His friend Sherwood lay curled there, still as death. Cold crept from Lowry's fingertips throughout his body until even his lips felt numb. A great buzz filled his ears and everything went black.

Something brushed his cheek and he opened his eyes. He was

stretched flat on the ground and Father was leaning over him, shaking his shoulder. Lowry saw Father's mouth move, but he could hear no words. Dimly he knew that something was wrong, that he must get up. Then he remembered with shock: Sherwood! He rolled groggily to his knees and struggled slowly to his feet. Father offered him a steadying hand before turning to tend once again to the young slave.

As Father knelt and tenderly lifted Sherwood's limp body, giving no thought to his own white shirt, which quickly became stained with the boy's blood, a string of curse words drew Lowry's attention to the whip-wielding stranger. He had mounted his horse and was jeering from a safe distance.

"That'll learn you to truck with slaves and teach 'em to read! You ain't the only one as can teach lessons. Run him home to his master and tell him, if you dare! You can't be everywheres at once. If I catch that boy out here again, I'll finish the job!" Father's expression was bleak as the man spurred his horse and cantered away.

"Is Sherwood—" Lowry's voice cracked. Father said nothing but hurried toward Mr. Roberts' plantation. Sherwood's head lolled against Father's arm as he carried him down the path. Lowry trotted woodenly behind them. It was unbearable not to know. He burst out, "Oh, Father, is Sherwood dead?"

"No, son. He's alive, though just." Father could barely speak. "That man is right. I cannot be everywhere at once. Mr. Roberts will have to send Sherwood away."

"But, Father!" Lowry sniffled. He was crying in earnest now. "Sherwood's my friend!"

"Yes, he is your friend, so you must help me. Run and tell Mother what has happened. She'll know what to do."

"Yes, sir." He felt better for having something to do, but he hesitated. "Will I see Sherwood again?"

"No, son. He is not safe here. Don't worry about him, Lowry.

God is everywhere at once, and he will take care of Sherwood. Run on now!"

Still in shock, Lowry whispered, "Good-bye, Sherwood." He stumbled blindly for home. He tried not to think, but suddenly the realization was there—this was slavery. He stopped and dragged his sleeve across his eyes. A slave might have a good, kind master and be happy like Sherwood, but it could all change in the twinkling of an eye. Even a good man like Father could not control slavery. At last, Lowry understood why Father had left Tennessee, and why he wanted to leave Kentucky now.

He ignored the stitch in his side as his feet pummeled the path. If Sherwood was as good as gone, then there was nothing left to keep Lowry here in Kentucky. He never wanted to see anyone suffer like that again. He had to get away from slavery forever. He had to get to Ohio.

Chapter 2

LOWRY SHIVERED AS HE watched the ice-choked Ohio River flowing past the muddy embankment where he stood. He looked across to the village of Ripley in Brown County, Ohio, thinking about the events of the past few months and wondering what the future might hold. Tomorrow would be the first day of 1826. Colonel Pogue had invited Father to preach in Ripley on Sunday, and to stay there with him until he could build a house if Father should be called to serve the congregation. Last night, the Rankins had lodged near the ferry in Augusta, Kentucky. This morning, Mr. Courtney, the ferryman, had startled them with his timetable for crossing over to Ripley.

"I tell you, I've lived on the river many years and you must cross today. We'll be perfectly safe. The skiffs will easily travel between the chunks of ice, if we hurry," he assured Father.

Lowry saw Mother dart a wide-eyed glance at the icy river, then at her children. Ibby sang to baby Calvin as he yawned. David watched the gray clouds spit snow, but Lowry jigged with impatience. The sooner Kentucky and everything to do with slavery was behind them, the sooner life could get back to normal. He hoped Father would not hesitate and ruin everything.

"If we don't go now, you won't be able to cross for many days." Mr. Courtney played on their hesitation like a shopkeeper losing a sale. He had the anxious look of a man who did not want to board the Rankins until April. Lowry held his breath and waited for Father's answer.

Father turned to look at Mother. Her wide gray eyes showed

her exhaustion. Worry lines creased her forehead as she jostled baby Calvin. Straggles of brown hair escaped from her bonnet and the limp ribbons flapped in the breeze. Her cheeks were gaunt and her hands were chapped. It had taken a weary long time to settle debts and to say good-byes, and then Mother had supervised as Father packed all their belongings into one wagon and jounced uphill and down to the Ohio. It taxed her strength just to nod her head and murmur, "All right, Mr. Courtney. We shall go now."

Lowry's heart skipped a beat. At last, he would be shut of Kentucky! He tried not to think about Sherwood. Within minutes, but not fast enough for Lowry, Mr. Courtney's son filled one skiff with most of the housekeeping necessities as Mother directed. The Rankins' horse and most of their goods they left with the Courtneys to hold until spring. Courtney's son launched his craft and was halfway across the river before Lowry had gingerly settled himself in the other skiff.

"Now, ain't this fine?" Mr. Courtney observed. Lowry shot a triumphant glance at Father when he heard Mr. Courtney's grammar, but Father did not appear to notice. Instead, he doled out an alarming pile of coins and the ferryman pushed off from the shore.

The skiff raced faster than Lowry had ever traveled in his life. He wanted to shout! He squinted to keep the hard pellets of snow out of his eyes. The snow stung like fire, but the river ice mesmerized him. The floes looked like chilly stepping-stones—why, he could almost walk across them to the other side. He watched as a faraway field of ice, as wide as two tabletops but twice as thick, sailed along on the current like a wispy cloud on the wind. They were racing it, and winning! He laughed aloud and swiveled to watch Mr. Courtney as he deftly threaded the skiff between the dirty gray blocks of ice.

Lowry looked back again, and this time his heart was gripped with fear. He opened his mouth to cry out but he could not make a sound. The table of ice was rushing at the skiff and would strike it in seconds, and only Lowry knew it. He sounded like a weak kitten as he squeaked, "Look out!"

"Hold on!" Mr. Courtney roared. With one desperate sweep of his arm, Father grabbed Lowry, Ibby, and David and yanked them to his side. Lowry's mouth smashed against Father's collarbone and he tasted salt where his teeth cut into his lower lip. He tried to draw a deep breath but Father's embrace was too tight. The skiff shuddered and creaked ominously as the ice floe rammed the hull. Then everything whirled.

The ice lodged under the skiff and spun it halfway around until it reared like a fractious colt. Lowry's scalp prickled as the whole world tilted and the household bundles tumbled slowly backward. His feet dangled toward the brown, swirling water despite Father's deathly firm grip. His breakfast was nudging at the back of his throat when he heard a tremendous splash and the boat rocked off the ice and back into the water. Lowry's entire body went limp with relief.

He watched dazedly as the ice table bucketed down the river. Gradually, the skiff stopped rocking and his breakfast settled back in his stomach. He dabbed at his bloody lip and looked at Mother, who sat with a hand to her chest as baby Calvin squalled. Father rubbed a splash of muddy water from his cheek, smoothed his hair, and cleared his throat. "Mr. Courtney!" His chin came up and his lips pressed together in a thin line.

"Yes, sir?" Mr. Courtney's words stretched mournfully. Lowry felt sorry for the man, whose face was an interesting shade of apple green.

"Thank you." Father clapped him on the shoulder. "You did well. We'll sleep in a free state this New Year's Eve." He smiled, and all the sternness melted from his countenance.

Mr. Courtney straightened his back and beamed at Father.

He set his cap at a jaunty angle and rowed the Rankins to their new life across the wide river.

Spring arrived much later in Ohio than in Kentucky, Lowry noticed. Of all the disagreeable effects of the weather, he had thought ice was the worst, but a good argument could be made for mud. Mud slowed everything down, made every move sluggish and heavy. As the spring showers dragged into summer downpours, Lowry thought that Father would never finish the new house in the brief gaps between all his pastoral duties. The scarlet leaves of the sugar maples covered the ground again before the weather cleared for good. The sun beamed pleasantly the day the Rankins moved from their rented house to their new home at 224 Front Street. The plain, red-brick, two-story house was sixty feet wide and thirty feet deep.

The size of the house gave the town wags a reason to shake their heads. "Someone needs to teach Pastor Rankin to manage his money better. Why does a minister need a big, fancy house with three front doors? Who ever heard of such a thing?" The talk spread like wildfire that the new pastor was a crazy spendthrift.

Lowry was embarrassed, but Father instructed him to ignore the gossip. "A man can hardly support a family of four—no, five children, counting new baby Samuel, on my salary, but that's what I must do, and build a house, too, Lowry," he explained. "In truth, I built three houses, not one, all under the same roof. Three families need three doors," he smiled. "We will occupy the third one at the end and hope to find another family to rent the center one at fifty dollars a year. David Ammen, the editor of the *Castigator*, has already agreed to rent the other end, with his family downstairs and his Ramage printing press upstairs." Father flexed his shoulders. "Though I am tuckered out right now, I know I shall be well paid for my labor. Ammen says we may swap rent for publishing privileges in the future. For now, his friendship will suffice, and the extra money is welcome." When Father explained matters, everything made perfect sense.

Lowry liked Ripley, which had tucked itself into a pretty bend of the Ohio River. The houses stood in a stiff row along Front Street, like the paper doll chains that Ibby cut from heavy paper. Behind the other streets, a narrow ribbon of sun-bleached grass trimmed the base of a steep, crumbly bluff that rose to brush the sky. He admired the village as he walked to school with Father one morning late in October.

As they drew abreast of a tavern, two drunken men lurched into the street. One stood squarely in Father's path with a smirk on his face. The other splattered the ground at Lowry's feet with tobacco juice.

"We don't want none of your religion here. Why don't you go back where you came from?" The man glowered at Father.

"Good morning, sir. Come to church on Sunday and I'll answer your question," Father replied in his precise manner.

"We ain't coming to church, you—" The second man launched a stream of filthy language at Father, who proceeded with unruffled dignity. Lowry's ears tingled; he shrank down in his shoes and tried to hide.

"Here, you, leave the minister alone! He's worth two of you! Go along before I knock your heads together!" A man the size of a bear—or so it always seemed to Lowry—emerged from a nearby storefront. Mr. Patton, a deacon at the church, loomed protectively over Father and Lowry until the ruffians staggered away. "Ho, ho, ho!" he laughed after them. "You won't see them for a month of Sundays, Pastor Rankin!"

"That is just when a pastor might do them the most good, Robert," Father replied a trifle sadly.

The big man shook with laughter and slapped his knee. Lowry

smiled as he thought of what the boys in town called Mr. Patton. The nickname "Jolly Bob" suited him well. With a cheery wave, the deacon ducked into the feed store.

Father shook his head in disgust when they were out of earshot of the drunkards. "That's what comes of selling whiskey almost as cheap as water. A quarter a gallon!" Father snorted. "Men, women, and even children are guzzlin' liquor. Families starve, and some men sell their wives' dresses off their backs to buy a jug." Father stopped abruptly and shook his finger in Lowry's face. "See that you never touch a drop of alcohol, Lowry."

Lowry nodded. Father seemed as tall as a tree when he gave an order. Lowry dared not disobey him; he did not see how those drunkards could. He turned up his nose. Anyone could see that Father was a better man than those common fellows were. He always wore a spotless white stock and a neat black frock coat. His high-colored, handsome face was cleanly shaven and his dark hair neatly brushed. Why, Father was a minister! His words slashed at sin like a double-edged sword. The last thing Lowry wanted was to argue with him. Father was always right, and the people of Ripley might as well get used to it.

He picked up a smooth stone and skipped it across the surface of the Ohio River. The path to school bordered the waterway that meant everything to the town. After all, that was how the steamboats traveled, and they were still enough of a novelty in Ripley that every man, woman, and child in town turned out to watch with curiosity as the steamers passed majestically up and down the river.

Store goods came by the river, like the latest fashions from New York and Philadelphia, or sugar and molasses from the plantations down in New Orleans. The scrambling slaves in their gaily striped suits of jeans could never unload the goods fast enough to satisfy the captains. When the river froze, people had to resort to tedious overland travel, which slowed everything down. Lowry knew all he cared to about traveling on icy rivers. Besides, even the roads were cut to follow the river's course. The Ohio River affected Ripley every minute of every day, especially the town's business.

If the Ohio rose, the town had better pay attention; a flood could mean disaster. Danger loomed when the water was low, as well. A steamboat might strike a snag and delay the delivery of precious cargo.

Ripley sent pork up the river to Pittsburgh, where it was re-shipped to eastern cities, and down the river to New Orleans. Ohio farmers mostly raised hogs as their livestock, and mostly corn as their crop. They killed two birds with one stone when it came time to sell: "I let my corn walk to market!" the farmers bragged. Lowry never ceased to marvel at all the hogs that ambled through town. Drovers and dogs herded the heedless animals from all points in Ohio to two places. Cincinnati ranked first in pork packing, but Ripley shouldered in for second place. Hogs thronged the muddy streets that led to Thomas McCague's slaughterhouse.

At McCague's, they not only butchered and dressed out the hogs, but they also put rendered lard into kegs and packed pickled pork into barrels. Lowry could not stomach a visit to the wharf. There, cured hams, shoulders, and sides of bacon lay unpacked and unprotected until stevedores stacked the products every which way on the boats, like random blocks. One day, Lowry saw a dog gnawing at a slab, and he never ate pork without remembering that.

Pork was understandably not Lowry's favorite supper, but the hog trade had made Thomas McCague the wealthiest man in Ohio. The jovial Kentuckian and his stately wife, Kittie, were friends with everyone in Ripley and beyond. They had beautiful manners, and it amused Lowry that their genteel demeanor was in such stark contrast to the deportment of the hogs on which they made their money. He chuckled to see a hog stop and slobber in delight as it gobbled up an apple core from the street. It took some getting used to, all the trash that people would throw in the middle of Main Street, but there was no place else to put the refuse. Anyway, the hogs greedily snatched it up, and there were always more lean hogs coming to town to fatten up on the garbage.

Of course, when the hogs passed through, they left pungent calling cards, and Lowry watched his step every minute. He preferred to walk on the sidewalks made out of warped boards, nailed crossways, side by side. Even the sidewalks were difficult for Mother and Ibby to navigate. The hems of the women's long skirts forever snagged in the cracks between the rough boards, but the ladies minded that less than stepping through hog manure up to six inches deep.

To be fair, the hogs were not the only offenders. Lowry bet that one horse could easily add twenty pounds of manure to the streets a day. He had mucked out enough stalls to make a good guess, and there were many horses in Ripley. Dogs, cats, and chickens, too—it all added up.

Mother and Ibby mostly avoided walking through town. The only time they enjoyed the trip was after a heavy rain, something it seemed Mother prayed for almost daily during the summer. When she craved a good clean rain to freshen the ripe air, she prayed for a sod-soaker. A gully-washer was even better in her eyes, for then it rained hard enough to wash away the manure and litter from the low places where it tended to collect. The best rain was a deluge of biblical proportions, the kind Mother called a trash-mover. A downpour like that tumbled everything in its path down the streets and into the river, even the carcasses of dead horses or cows that no one bothered to bury.

There were drawbacks to heavy rain, though. Liquid mud made the streets impassable, so Father had to leave his horse at home for a while. After the mud dried up, the whole mess started over again. A drought was just as bad, Lowry reflected. During a long dry spell, the women held handkerchiefs to their noses and shooed away the swarms of flies that buzzed around the offal rotting in the streets. No wonder Mother's eyes watered whenever she ventured into Ripley, and no wonder she always scuttled quickly back into the house. What a stink! Dr. Campbell even speculated that the ripe air could cause cholera. Lowry did not know about that.

"Morning, John! Morning, Lowry!"

Lowry and Father tipped their hats to Dr. Campbell as they passed the public well in front of his grand white house at 114 Front Street. Lowry liked the doctor, because he never put on airs, even though he might soon be governor of Ohio. He was talking with a man whom Lowry did not know but Father seemed to.

"How are you, Thomas?" Father bellowed, putting his mouth close to the other man's ear.

The man jumped when Father spoke. "Yes, I'm Thomas Collins—oh, hello, John! What's that you said?" Under his shock of flaxen hair, he had a kind face and rosy cheeks. He cupped a brown-stained hand to his ear. Lowry's jaw dropped. Father had used his Sunday voice and the man had not heard him.

Father clapped him on the shoulder. "Good day!" he shouted and tipped his hat.

"Good day to you, sir!" Relief spread across Mr. Collins's face. He filled his bucket at the well and walked to the cabinetmaker's shop at 200 Front Street. Well, that explained the stains on the man's fingers.

"Father—" Lowry began.

"Mr. Collins is hard of hearing, son. We must be considerate of those less fortunate."

Lowry screwed up his face. "But, Father, how can he do business if he—"

"Mr. Collins's main trade is in coffins, son."

"Coffins!" Lowry exclaimed. A warning glance from Father silenced him. Well, Lowry guessed that Mr. Collins's hearing loss would not bother him much in *that* trade.

The thought of choosing a trade made Lowry's stomach do a flip-flop. What would he be, one day? He thought about all the men he had seen this morning: Dr. Campbell, who might one day be a governor; "Jolly Bob" Patton, a deacon and a farmer; Mr. Collins, a practically deaf cabinetmaker who made coffins; and Mr. McCague, a wealthy hog butcher. To be fair, there was Father, too, a minister. Lowry sighed. He had no interest in any of those trades. How could those men abide the same tedious work day after day? At least they did their own work, he reasoned. Those who had once owned slaves had freed them long before Father came to town.

Mr. Ammen, the newspaper editor who rented part of Father's house, now *his* job sounded fine. He was a lucky man, working with that wonderful Ramage printing press all day. Lowry never got tired of watching him set type. Mr. Ammen had even let Lowry help with the press while he printed Father's letters to Uncle Thomas Rankin. Father had carefully saved every letter to his youngest brother, because he had worked so hard to convince him to set his slaves free. Uncle Thomas did set them free, to Father's joy. Father and Mr. Ammen thought other people should read those letters, too, so Mr. Ammen was printing them in book form. The press reproduced the letters ever so much faster than Father could write them by hand.

Work-saving machines fascinated Lowry. Over the summer, he had worked in the Ripley woolen mill, splicing rolls on the spinning machine for twelve and a half cents a day. At home, he had even designed a miniature inclined wheel and hitched up the uncooperative family cat to power it. The concept of saving time pleased Lowry, but his chiefest pleasure came when he watched the big machines whirring and clacking in precision.

When Lowry and Father arrived at the corner of Second and Market streets, a tattered ball landed at their feet. Lowry nudged it with his toe. Many times back in Kentucky he had wound rags around a walnut, or even a stone, to make a padded ball like this one. He picked it up, hefted it thoughtfully, and a grin of pure pleasure spread across his face. Time enough to think of trades one day. A busy year of building and hard work had gone by without a chance to meet many Ripley boys, just the few that attended church. Now Lowry needed to fit in at a new school, and it would be fun to play with boys his own age again. "Throw it back, will you?" one coaxed. Lowry grinned and tossed the ball to a snaggle-toothed boy with red hair, and the noisy game of Annie Over resumed in the schoolyard.

"Can you run fast?" the redhead hollered. Lowry nodded. "He's on our side!" the boy announced. "Come on!"

Without a backward glance at Father, Lowry dashed to the schoolhouse steps and carefully set down Pike's Arithmetic and the English Reader, books that he brought from home. He sprinted to the far side of the one-room log schoolhouse at the redhead's heels. "You know how to play?" the boy panted.

"Mm-hmm." Lowry wasted no words. He noticed that his team had fewer boys than the other team—that meant they were losing. Here was a chance to prove himself. Lowry had won many a game of Annie Over in Kentucky. He might be small for being almost ten, but he could run like a blue streak, and if you could catch a ball and run fast, you could win at Annie Over.

The redhead's hair flashed like fire in the sun as he heaved the ball high over the schoolhouse roof. "Annie, Annie over!" he shouted. The ball disappeared over the peak and clattered down the other side. Lowry watched the sides of the schoolhouse warily until he heard "Annie, Annie over!" from the other side. He knew that meant no one had caught the ball on the fly, and sure enough, it whizzed back over the ridge and rolled off the eaves, ten feet above the ground. Now was his chance. The ball took a wicked hop off the edge but he snatched it in midair. He dashed around the building with his whole team following in a silent pack hot on his heels. If only they could take the other team by surprise!

They caught them staring in flat-footed apprehension at the roof. Lowry tagged the closest boy, and he was captured for Lowry's team. He tagged two more boys before they could escape to safety at the other side of the building. Just like that, Lowry's team was back in the game. They all whooped and slapped his shoulders, and Lowry caught a glimpse of Father as he left the schoolyard. He waved and turned back to the game.

"That your pa?" a captured boy from the other team asked. He was quite a bit bigger than the other boys. Lowry's head just about reached his chest.

"Uh-huh," he said. "He's the preacher. Say, what time does school commence?"

The giant stared at Lowry with his mouth hanging open. "What did you say?"

"What time does school commence?"

"Did you hear that?" the boy guffawed to the others. "'Whut tahm does school cum-MEE-yince?'" he drawled. He rubbed his stubbly jaw. "Where are you from, anyway?"

"Kentucky." A gone feeling shot through Lowry. What had he done, he wondered, to make this half-grown-mountain of a boy laugh at him? As a knot of gleeful boys gathered, Lowry turned to walk away.

"Say something else, Kentucky boy," the ringleader taunted.

"Why? I talk plain, same as y'all."

"He talks 'pline,' he says. Haw, haw, haw! 'You-all' hear that?"

Lowry set his teeth and refused to say another word. A shrewd light crept into his tormentor's pig-like eyes. "Your preacher pa loves slaves, don't he? Where'd you get your curly yellow hair? Maybe your ma was a slave," he crooned.

That did it. Lowry tore into the big boy with both fists. The next thing he knew, he was lying flat on his face with the breath knocked out of him and one arm twisted up behind his back—and it hurt. He felt like a draft horse had tromped on him until his insides were ground to a pulp.

"You leave him alone, Luke Means! Why do you come to school, anyway? You're thirteen already, and you don't want to learn!" A tiny black shoe stamped near Lowry's face. Suddenly his arm was free. He heard a thump and a froth of white petticoat and blue-striped cotton dusted the ground beside him.

"Luke Means!" A male voice roared the name; Lowry guessed it must be the teacher. "For pushing a girl, you may go home, sir, and don't come back to school! I'll have the law on you if you do!"

"If I do go home, it's because I want to, not because you or a snot-faced girl tells me to. I can make good money right now, patrolling the river for raggedy runaway slaves and running them back to their masters. What do I need school for?" Luke Means clomped away, his departure punctuated by a string of growled curses.

Air seeped back into Lowry's lungs, but his ribs ached. He buried his face in the crook of his arm and wished he could disappear into a hole in the ground. Slavery again! Would he never escape it?

"Are you all right?" The owner of the striped cotton dress stood next to him as she smoothed her skirts.

Then and there, Lowry decided not to speak at school that day unless a teacher spoke to him. He nodded his head; it hurt too much to move anything else.

"Can I help you any?" Doubt laced her voice.

Lowry wagged his head back and forth. The girl had already done enough. He did not want her to come to his rescue again.

"Well, all right. That Luke is a bad one. Sometimes I feel like I just have to *do* something, you know. School takes up in a minute, so you'd better come on." She chattered enough for both of them, Lowry thought.

The girl sashayed toward the building. Curiosity overcame Lowry's discomfort and he peeped at his benefactress. Long golden ringlets lay in shining waves on her shoulders beneath her sunbonnet. She looked back once. She had a sweet face with very blue eyes that bored into Lowry's. She smiled.

"Come along, Mandy! Leave that Kentucky boy be." A taller girl shook her finger.

"I'm coming, Julie Ann, but you needn't think you can boss me just because you're the big sister. Mama said you mayn't."

As Mandy tripped into the schoolhouse, Lowry lay still for a moment before creaking to his feet like an old man. The schoolyard spun and he swayed, but gulps of fresh air could not cure him. A single smile and eyes as blue as cornflowers had muddled his senses more than any bully ever could.

Chapter 3

As fall gave way to winter, and winter crept into spring, Lowry got used to keeping mum. The other children teased him because he never talked except when Mr. Brockway called on him to recite. Occasionally, Amanda Kephart would stand up for him, just as she had when Luke Means tore into him on the first day. "He can't help it if he's shy!" she'd flash when the other boys made fun. Even if he were not already tongue-tied over his accent, he would have been mute around Amanda, anyway. Hopelessly smitten, he adored her silently from afar.

By the end of the next long summer, Lowry had come to believe that he actually *was* shy. When school took up again in the fall of 1827, his heart pounded whenever the teacher asked him a question. He looked down at his shoes and blushed, afraid his Kentucky accent would get him into trouble again. It did not help matters that he was now eleven but had not grown an inch. All the other boys had shot up and filled out their clothes, but Mother actually had to take in some of Lowry's breeches.

"I'm worried about him, John. He's like a scarecrow. He never smiles, and can you imagine Lowry *shy*?" Mother's knitting needles clacked indignantly in the parlor. "Mr. Brockway spoke of it in town today."

On the stairs, Lowry squirmed in embarrassment. Sleet scoured the window behind him. The landing was too chilly for sitting there in his nightclothes, but he had to know what else Mr. Brockway had said. His shivered and hugged his knees as he eavesdropped.

"I've asked Isabella, and she said that after the fight with that overgrown bully, Luke Means, on the first day, which was unfortunate but only to be expected in a town like this, Lowry has never been in another altercation. I don't think the trouble lies entirely there."

A newspaper rustled as Father turned the page. "Perhaps he just needs a sense of duty."

In the silence that followed, Lowry could hear the flames crackling on the hearth and the clock ticking away the minutes.

"A sense of duty?" Mother said. "What on earth do you mean? No, I think this town is too rough a place for him. He was always so happy in Kentucky, until the trouble with Sherwood, that is."

Lowry heard Mother sigh. Maybe she wanted to forget about slavery, too.

"Perhaps there is a means to accomplish both ends," Father replied. "We need a bigger house, a garden for our family, and a more private place away from—well, just away. You know the old Pogue place on the hill above town?"

Lowry leaned forward in stealthy excitement.

"Yes, but what does that have to do with Lowry?"

"Do you not think he would be happier if we moved to sixty-five and a half acres of land? It is heavily timbered and the soil is excellent, even though the land is unimproved," Father answered.

Mother's rocking chair creaked. "Move? Away from town? Oh, John!" Lowry remembered how she detested the taverns and the smells. He could hear the smile in her voice. "But it's unimproved, you say. Where would we live?"

"There are plenty of logs for a temporary house. We shall use that for a stable after we build a brick house." Father paused. "What do you think?"

Mother's voice warmed still more. "Why, I can set out a garden next spring, if we hurry! We can sell this apartment and build a house with room enough for our family. The Ammens can stay in their apartment, if they've a mind to. It will all work out, if God has plans for us up there. Lowry can have the run of the place, away from those bullies in town. Let's, John! Only . . . what about . . ." she hesitated. Lowry wondered what it was that she would not put into words.

"The situation is lovely," Father cut in smoothly. "To the south, we can see ten miles along the river and to the northeast, almost six miles. That's far enough to see a body coming quite a ways."

Mother and Father murmured on for so long that Lowry's head finally drooped. He awoke with a start to Father's gentle shaking of his shoulder. "Come along, Lowry. Time enough to hear about our new home tomorrow. Off to bed." Drowsily, he wondered if Father had known all along he was on the stairs.

With the help of a few good friends in town, Father quickly knocked together a rude log house and the Rankins took up residence on the ridge. Next, Father collected an old debt from someone back in Carlisle—a load of bricks he had bartered in exchange for the house the family had left behind there. Ever so slowly, the new house took shape along the ridge, just above where it sloped down to the town. Once the framing was done, Lowry thought he would never tire of watching as Father laid the red brick. The stretchers were set longways and the headers shortways to make a pleasing pattern.

From the first floor to the second, and from the attic to the cellar, Father's attention to detail showed. Lowry could not decide which part of the house he liked best. The white, six-panel front door opened between two white columns, looking out across the river to Kentucky. Above the door, a horizontal transom light of four windowpanes illumined the entry hall. A peaked raincap set on the top of the columns sheltered the transom from the rain. On either side of the door, a tall window was set in the middle of the wall, and above each one the bricks arched endways in a pretty fan.

The sides of the house had a window upstairs and one down, offset from each other. Four cast-iron stars marched along the line between the edges of the roof. Father explained that these were short wall-ties. He drove an iron bolt into a solid wooden crossbeam of the frame and laid the bricks so that the bolt protruded a bit from the wall. Then he threaded the bolt through a hole in the center of the cast-iron star, which acted as a washer to hold everything firmly in place. Four brick chimneys graced the front and back slopes of the roof, two on each side. The roof sloped lower at the back of the house to shade a wide back porch. Because it faced north, the porch would be a cool place to sit on warm summer evenings.

Early in 1828, the Rankin family finally moved into their new home, in plenty of time for Mother to set out a garden, just as she had predicted. Inside, four rooms lined a center hall downstairs, with two big rooms upstairs. Long storage rooms were situated under the eaves.

Lowry loved to sit on the stone doorstep and look down the ridge—540 feet—to Ripley, where tiny horses and miniature people scurried among the toy houses. He had a bird's-eye view of the sparkling Ohio River, which flowed almost due north toward the ridge before it curved off to the east. Across the river, farmhouses flanked by cedar groves dotted the sculpted emerald fields. He could see Asa Anderson's farmstead, a mirror image of the Rankin farm on the Kentucky side. At twilight, the slow, lazy ripples of the Ohio reflected the deep aqua of the sky as the sun sank behind the Kentucky hills.

By March, when the pussy willow catkins dotted the swampy lowlands in town, a good bit of timber on the hill had been nibbled back, enlarging the clearing around the house. All spring, the sound of axes rang through the air. Great trees tottered and swooned slowly to the ground like ladies with the vapors, leafy green skirts trailing carelessly behind. Hired men split and tossed wood into a little ox cart as the redbuds colored the hills a deep pink. Lowry carted the firewood to sell to the steamboats or to townsfolk.

Late one May afternoon, Mother had a job for Lowry. "Son, will you please take the wood cart to Pappaw's new house on Second Street?" She deftly jointed the last of six cleaned chickens and carefully salted and peppered every inch. Lowry knew that meant chicken pie for supper. Fascinated, he watched as she covered a deep dish with a thick doughy crust and doubled over the ends at the rim. She plopped two of the chickens in the dish, cut thick pats of butter, and dotted the meat with it. Her hands flew as she added more layers. "Remind him if he tries to pay that we're not likely to charge my father for firewood!" She put the last of the chicken and the last of a pound and a half of butter into the dish and covered it with the thick top crust. When she drew the pie from the oven in an hour and a half, she would open the crust and add gravy, but right now, she cut tiny slits in the raw dough with a sharp knife while a pleased smile played about her lips. Lowry knew she was happy her parents had moved to Ripley from Tennessee.

"Yes, Mother," Lowry replied. He wrinkled his nose. Here, then, was the duty that Father had spoken of—the same old chores, but more of them. He did not relish the thought of going back into town among all the people, and the gone feeling returned. Only the thought that he might catch a glimpse of Amanda Kephart cheered him. He squared his shoulders and kissed his mother's cheek. She smiled and told him to take a doughnut, which he stowed in his pocket for the walk home.

As he yoked the ponderous oxen, Lowry wondered just when he would look his age. Soon he would be twelve, yet strangers still chucked him under the chin and spoke in simpering tones normally reserved for small children, if they addressed him at all. What good was being eleven if no one could tell?

Finished with the hitching up, Lowry stood straight and tall on the team's off side. Early sunshine blazed on his shoulders; it was mighty hot for May. He noticed for the first time that the redbud blossoms were strewn over the ground beneath the trees. One early daisy nodded in the breeze, but for the most part, the eyes of the daisies were still squeezed shut. The heady scent of red clover sweetened the air, driving the honeybees to distraction as they sipped and dined. One white cloud drifted across the arching blue sky, but Lowry's feet dragged as he drove the oxen down the steep, roundabout track to town. The wood rattled and clattered in the cart as Lowry shouted, "Gee!" or "Haw!" and used his goad to carefully guide the team.

"Whoa-a-a." Lowry halted the team in the narrow alley behind Pappaw's house. He stacked the wood while the blunt-nosed red oxen patiently stood. He had made a considerable dent in the load before Pappaw caught him at it.

"Bill!" Pappaw called. Then he addressed his namesake. "Well, Lowry, you're 'most done," he congratulated. "Why don't you stretch your legs and deliver a message to Mr. McCague for me? Your Uncle Bill will help me finish."

Lowry smirked and nodded. Bill, who was Mother's youngest brother, was only six weeks older than Lowry himself. He straightened slowly, happy for both the praise and the chance to stop. "All right, Pappaw," Lowry answered quietly. If any of the town boys heard him use the Kentucky word for grandpa, he would be a goner. "When I come back, I'll help him finish stacking."

He wandered back down the alley and turned on Mulberry Street toward Front. He kept his eyes peeled for golden ringlets and cornflower-blue eyes, but he saw no sign of Amanda at the hotel her father kept on Front Street. Just then, Lowry heard a burst of loud jeers from the direction of the riverbank. He skirted Mr. McCague's house on the river and crested the bank, curious but cautious.

Down below, he saw a crowd of men dawdling on the wharf. A raft of saw logs floated just offshore, and a slave man toiled at the remaining logs as his master sold them. Lowry recognized the slave's owner, Matthias James. He was a Kentuckian from just upriver, and everyone called him Tice for short. Lowry saw Luke Means sidle up to Mr. James. Luke was a river patroller now, and as he spoke to Mr. James, Lowry's mouth felt like it was stuffed full of cotton. He had no desire to see Luke again. He ducked into Mr. McCague's enormous lilac bush, which was crowded with fragrant lavender spikes. There he watched and listened, unobserved.

"You better keep an eye on your man, Tice," Luke drawled. "He's gonna jump off and head for the woods." He licked his thick lips and smiled in anticipation.

Mr. James glared at Luke and swore, and Lowry cringed. The Kentuckian said, "Well, you sure would hunt him down and earn twenty-five dollars off me, wouldn't you? Are you trying to encourage my man to take his foot in hand, Random Means?" Lowry mustered a tiny grin at hearing Mr. James call Luke by his nickname, a play on the boy's last name and his money-grubbing ways.

"I'm not saying nothin' save you better watch 'im," Luke rejoined. "Can you afford to lose another slave this month? Let's see, three have run off so far," he gloated, his little piggy eyes gleaming under the tousled mat of black hair.

Matthias James's face turned brick red. "See here, Random! If this one runs off, I can sure enough catch him myself. I can outrun any slave in Kentucky, catch him by the nape of his neck like a pup, and drag him back with his tail tucked between his legs! I don't need you to tell me how to attend to my business!"

For the first time, the black man registered that he'd overheard the exchange. Lowry saw him steal a sidelong glance at his master, a calculating look. Then he hustled along, grappling the logs off the raft even faster, grunting as he worked.

"So you can outrun any slave in Kentucky, Tice?" a heckler called out.

"Yes, sir, I can!" Mr. James shot back. His eyes nearly popped from his head and a bulge of veins mapped his temple. Lowry grinned to see him so flustered.

"Well, where do you suppose you are right now, Tice?" another persisted.

By now, Mr. James had had enough. He hurled down his tools and turned to face the crowd with murder in his eyes.

"I'll tell you where you are, Tice, my friend!" shouted a good-humored voice from the high front porch at 212 Front Street.

Mr. James swung around to locate the source of this latest remark. When he saw who it was, his face softened so much that he looked as kind as Pappaw. "And where might that be, Tom McCague, you old scoundrel?"

"Why, my friend, you are in Ohio, and a more inhospitable place I've never known. I wish that I might go back with you to Kentucky, my homeland, where the air is pure and the people are civil." Mr. McCague talked as if Kentucky was hundreds of miles away, instead of just across the river. He smiled broadly as he descended his front steps before disappearing from view for a few seconds as he stepped down into the yard, hidden by the seven-foot-high board fence that enclosed his property. Then the high gate swung open and the hog dealer crossed over to the lilac bush where Lowry was hiding. The gate slammed shut with a bang and Lowry heard the latch fall.

The crowd relaxed, and Mr. James actually smiled. Everyone along the river knew Mr. Thomas McCague, the wealthiest man in Ohio. All called him friend, regardless of personal politics.

Finished now with his business, Mr. James turned toward his friend, ready to jaw a while longer. With a guilty twinge, Lowry remembered the note from Pappaw. He wriggled from his sweetly scented fortress to deliver the missive, but stopped short when he saw the slave sail toward the shore in a tremendous leap. Lowry held his breath. Would he make it? Sure enough, the man cleared the edge of the river and then some, thumping to the ground on the steep, slippery slope and scrambling up the bank like a cat out of water.

"Tice, look!" Mr. McCague shouted. Startled, Mr. James whirled in time to see the slave reach the top of the embankment. He snarled and tried to make the shore with one long step, but the raft pushed away from the shore and his foot squelched into mud. With a mighty effort, he pulled his boot free and clambered lopsidedly up the rise.

The idle bystanders came to life. "Go to it, boy! Run, white man!" they cheered, parting to let the slave run through. That made the chase more sporting. Lowry saw the men surround Mr. James as he strained to keep one eye on the slave. Angrily he shoved bodies out of his way. Now the odds evened and the men took sides, urging on their favorites like it was a horse race. Lowry was so caught up in the excitement that it took a moment before he realized that the slave was sprinting directly toward him.

Everything slowed as he watched what happened next. Mr. McCague shouted again, raised his arm, and pointed. Mr. James followed Mr. McCague's pointing finger and looked away from the slave. Behind the lilac bush where Lowry hid, a plank of Mr. McCague's seven-foot-high board fence swung to the right on the top nail. He saw a high-button shoe nudge the board aside to allow a narrow passageway through the fence, but he doubted that anyone could see it beyond the lilacs. The slave topped the rise barely in time to see Mr. McCague jerk his head. It took forever for the runaway to reach the opening in the fence, but at last, he squeezed through practically under Lowry's nose. The plank shilly-shallied back into place. Before he could think, Lowry popped out of the lilac bush and took two steps toward Mr. McCague. As the gleeful mob and the angry slave owner swarmed into view, Lowry handed the startled hog dealer the note from Pappaw.

"Hey, Tice, did you catch him?" Mr. McCague cried.

Mr. James looked wildly about as he reached the place where Lowry and Mr. McCague stood, but the slave was nowhere to be seen. "Where'd he go, McCague?" he panted. "I was right on his miserable tail! Where's he hiding?" As he spoke, Mr. James sized up the landscape, looking for possible hiding places. He elbowed past Lowry and ripped apart the branches of the lilac bush. Fragrant purple stars scattered and their overpowering sweetness wafted incongruously over the commotion. Next, Mr. James seized the gate handle, but the latch held. He pounded the solid fence in frustration.

"Why, man, did you see him come by here? I thought sure you had time to grab the lazy brute," Mr. McCague protested.

Mr. James whipped his head around to stare hard at Mr. McCague. "Thomas McCague, do you or do you not know where he is?" he asked again, gasping for breath.

"Tice, I give you my word as a Kentucky gentleman that I saw you right on his heels, but I couldn't say where your man is now." Mr. McCague raised his hands, palms up and fingers outspread, and shook his head helplessly.

The tension stretched unbearably between the two men until Luke Means stepped from the far edge of the perplexed group of men. "You have to ask it right to get a straight answer. Ask that Rankin boy if he's seen your slave," he suggested, his expression shrewd.

All eyes turned to Lowry, who flinched. For a moment, he was back in the schoolyard with the bully who had trounced him on his first day. His heart thumped so loud in his chest that he felt sure everyone must hear it. "Well, boy, have you seen my slave?" roared Mr. James.

Lowry forced himself to look Mr. James in the eye. "Yes, sir, I saw him," he croaked. His cheeks grew hot. "I saw him on your raft." The men in the crowd snickered, but Mr. James glared at him. Lowry knew he had to *do* something. He raised his eyebrows, looked past Mr. James to a copse of nearby willows, and hoped Luke would take the bait.

Sure enough, Luke followed his glance and slouched off toward the trees with a sly smile. Before Lowry could escape, too, Mr. James grabbed his shoulder and shook him.

"See here, stop your foolin' around. You know what I meant! Come now, your pa don't hold with slavin', and you're like him, ain't ye? Where's my man?" the slave owner bellowed.

It was too much. Lowry's lips trembled and a tear rolled down his cheek. He swallowed the lump in his throat. "I don't know where he is now, sir!"

"Now, now, Tice, don't take it out on the boy." Mr. McCague gently pried Mr. James's fingers from Lowry's shoulder. Then he addressed the crowd. "You all know Mr. James always pays well when he gets a slave back. Do you want Random to get the money yet again? For there he goes!" Mr. McCague gestured toward the willows as Luke slunk through the shadows like a bloodhound on a hot trail.

"Hi, Means, not this time!" one man cried.

"Not if I can help it!" yelled another. The crowd seethed toward the trees with Mr. James in pursuit.

Mr. McCague watched them out of sight. A wry smile curved his mouth. "They'll all be over at the tavern for hours, planning who looks where." Then he looked down at Lowry with respect. "Tough as rawhide and Johnny-on-the-spot, aren't you?" he remarked quietly. He rested a comforting hand on Lowry's shoulder.

Lowry drew a shaky breath. "Not really, sir. I was just unloading wood at Pappaw's when he asked me to bring y'all the note, and well—"

"You must go back to your Pappaw's house," Mr. McCague

cut in smoothly, tousling Lowry's hair. "I allow he is waiting for you."

Lowry started past Mr. McCague, but the man stopped him. "This way." He guided Lowry through the front door to the back of the house. Kittie McCague, a tall woman in a dove-gray dress, stood in the kitchen. She removed a glass globe from a lamp in the window, and then lit a twist of paper at the stove. She cupped her hand around the flame, lit the candle, replaced the globe, and nodded at her husband.

"Hello, Adam Lowry, you scalawag," she winked. She whisked a folded paper into his hand. "Will you take this recipe to your mother for me? She asked me for it the other day."

"Good evening, Aunt Kittie. Of course," he answered politely. Every child in Ripley called her Aunt Kittie and loved her dearly. He took the paper and shoved it deep into his pocket.

Mr. McCague clearly had no time for Lowry to visit. He ushered him out the back door and led him to the rear fence. He swung another board aside and Lowry sidled through. Just like that, he was in his Pappaw's back yard, and Pappaw urged him to hurry through the house and into the front yard. Someone, maybe Bill, had pulled the ox cart out of the alley already, but it was still loaded with wood. Lowry shot a questioning glance at Pappaw, who shook his head.

"There's no time. Hurry home, Lowry. There could be trouble here later." He slapped the nigh ox's rump while Lowry puzzled over how Pappaw knew about the trouble with Mr. James. Then the cart lurched forward and he trotted alongside the oxen as the shadows lengthened.

What a strange day, he thought, as he guided the cart along Cornick's Run. Perhaps Aunt Kittie's nod meant that the slave lay hidden in the upper room of the McCague house. He knew that the McCagues helped runaway slaves, sometimes. Well, at least, he thought they did. No one ever talked about the runaways who passed through Ripley, and no one knew for sure who aided them. Lowry hoped his suspicion about the McCagues was correct, for if ever a slave deserved to escape, that fellow certainly did. Lowry bet he must have jumped twelve feet or more from the raft to shore. Mr. James's face had been a study.

Lowry almost stopped dead in his tracks when he thought of it. The candle! Dollars to doughnuts, the candle in the window was a signal to let somebody know that a slave needed help. He smiled triumphantly. To think he had figured out part of the mystery! The only question now was, who did the McCagues signal?

As long as he pondered the mystery, Lowry kept his courage up, but little worries soon crept into his thoughts like mice. Had there been some hidden meaning when Luke Means said, "Ask the Rankin boy if he's seen your slave"? He remembered how Luke had instantly followed his glance toward the willows, as if he counted on Lowry to give himself away. What if Luke was following him right now; or worse, if he was lying in wait up ahead, ready to jump Lowry and beat him up again? He shivered and said, "Get along!" to lift the oxen out of their plodding gait. He tried not to think about Luke. The creek murmured reassuringly as he prayed for safety. As an afterthought, he prayed for the slave, too.

At last, he pulled into the clearing. Father and Mother hurried out to meet him.

"You are late, Lowry," Mother stated, searching his face. Father reached for the oxen's yoke.

"Yes, Mother, I'm sorry. Pappaw sent me to Mr. McCague's with a note, and then Aunt Kittie sent you this recipe, too." He began to excuse his lateness, but he stopped and glanced down the hill. "Look!" he exclaimed, "See that candle in the McCague's window! I think I know why it's there!"

Mother paid him no attention. She studied the recipe with a

strange expression indeed. She showed the paper to Father, who read it, crumpled it, and put it into his pocket. A spasm made his jaw twitch. He held up a hand. "Quietly, Lowry. I do believe it is going to rain and voices carry," he cautioned.

Lowry lowered his voice impatiently and gestured to the cart. "But you'll never guess! Pappaw didn't get all his wood, because—"

"Because . . . " Father removed the logs quickly while Lowry watched. He saw Father reach deep into the pile of wood and grasp a hand. Thunderstruck, Lowry watched as Father helped Mr. James's runaway slave sit up in the cart. The man was gasping for breath.

Lowry's mouth dropped open and his eyes grew perfectly round. He, Lowry Rankin, had brought the slave away from town!

Suddenly Lowry did not care that he was small for his age, or that he spoke with a funny accent. He felt ten feet tall. Mr. McCague, Aunt Kittie, and Pappaw had trusted him to help a slave. They knew he could *do* something—and so did God, he reasoned. A warm glow started at his toes and spread to the roots of his hair. For a brief moment, he felt lifted above the world and saw it as God must, full of people connected to each other by a common bond—the bond of God's love.

Then a new idea niggled at him. Mr. McCague meant the candle as a signal for someone. Who else could that person be but Father?

Chapter 4

As if he could read Lowry's thoughts, Father spoke. "Remember, Lowry," he cautioned. "We must never speak outside the family about the people we aid. We do unto others as we would have them do unto us, but that's nobody's business but God's and ours. You have a new duty now, to this man here, and to many others like him." Father smiled and spoke to the runaway. "Come inside, sir, dinner's waiting. Don't be afraid. With the aid of kind Providence, you will soon be in a free country." The man stared at Father warily. He stood lopsided, as if something hurt him.

"But how will he get there?" Lowry asked.

"No time to explain now. Saddle up Old Sorrel and another horse, son. Get a large flour sack, too, and bring it with you." Lowry gaped at him. Surely, Father did not mean to send him to the gristmill after nightfall!

Lowry hated the long trip to the mill on Straight Creek. After a few hours, even a boy who loved machines tired of watching the monotonous motion of the mill wheel or the creaky grindstone. The miller thought nothing of making a boy wait forever for the wheat to be ground and bolted or sifted. Then Lowry had to ride home through the lonely woods in the dark.

"Now *I'm* being treated like a slave," he grumbled. He yanked the headstall over Old Sorrel's ears. There were only two things he wanted right now: his dinner, and to know how Father would get the runaway slave to safety.

He remembered the forgotten doughnut and retrieved it from his pocket. Biting into the still-tender crust, he chewed rapturously. There was nothing better than one of Mother's homemade doughnuts, even day old. Between bites he finished the tasks Father had given him.

When he strolled up to the house, he was licking the last rich crumbs from his fingers and feeling mellow. He tied Old Sorrel and the other horse to the fence and took the sack into the house. "Here you are, Father. You didn't tell me to fill the sack with wheat, so I didn't." The other children stared curiously at him, especially Ibby.

"Father, is Lowry going to the gristmill at night?" she asked.

"Ibby, you just run along upstairs, now, and take the rest of the children with you." Father's tone brooked no nonsense, and the younger children scurried. Lowry had the feeling they had not seen the fugitive yet, or they would not be so interested in what their brother was doing. He felt puffed with importance that he knew something they did not know.

Mother led Lowry to the kitchen, where the runaway sat shoveling down a steaming chicken pie. He held his spoon with his left hand, which curved awkwardly around the handle. Lowry shot an inquisitive look at the man who had made the long leap to shore. The man kept his right hand behind his back.

"Come here, Lowry. I want you to meet my friend," said Father.

Lowry's feet remained firmly planted. He felt the old, familiar shyness seize his tongue.

Father smiled encouragingly. "Lowry, this is David. David, don't be afraid. Lowry will not betray you." Father nudged him forward.

Lowry mumbled, "Howdy, David." He thrust out his right hand to shake.

Slowly David raised his head. He showed no emotion except in his eyes, which were deep brown pools of misery. His spoon clattered to the trencher and he extended his right hand.

Lowry gasped. David's fingers curled back toward his palm

like a crawdad's claw. He had no fingernails. Ridged lighter scars scored his wrists. He looked at David's face in shock. He wanted to see anything but that hand, but now he noticed for the first time a hideous necklace of scars around the man's neck, too.

"What happened?" Lowry forced the words out. He tried not to show his dismay.

David looked at Father, who nodded again. He began haltingly at first, but soon warmed to his story. "My master, Mr. James, he sold my wife and children away. When I run off to follow my family, he done caught me in town. He chain up my neck and fetter my hands and lead me off to the smithy's. He mad, so he hold my hand on the smithy's anvil and he club it with the hammer, but I don't make no sound. So he club it again and again." David paused, his expressive eyes far away, remembering. "Then he chain me by my neck to the back of his buggy. He whips up his horse to trot fast. Do I not run, he drag me by my neck, so I run behind, but I can't run as fast as a horse trots, no how." He rubbed at the rough scars on his neck, and Lowry felt a tear trickle down the side of his nose. "I run off ever' chance I get, but someone take me back ever' time," he added dejectedly.

Lowry hung his head. This was slavery. He recalled how he had grumbled about his trips to the gristmill and felt ashamed.

"It will not happen again." Father's eyes glinted dangerously. "Lowry will take you to the next safe house this very night. Many good men will escort you from one house to the next, all the way to Canada, and may God help you to find your wife and children safely when you arrive there."

David gaped, and so did Lowry. "You want *me* to take him?"

"Yes, son, ride with him to Archibald Hopkins's place. Mr. Hopkins will know what to do. Take the flour sack just for show."

Lowry's breath came in quick, excited gasps. "Father! Shall I hide him in the sack? He could curl up and hang over Old Sorrel's back, just like a sack of flour! Then I could—"

"No, Lowry." Father's voice was stern. "This is not a game. David is a grown man. We will treat him with the respect that God intended. If you keep your mind on business, you should have him over to Mr. Hopkins's holler in less than an hour. Take the bridle path." He turned to David. "I doubt that you'll meet anyone back there, but happen you do hear someone coming, slide off the horse and into the brush. Then Lowry will put the flour sack on your horse until it is safe for you to come out. Do you understand, Lowry?"

"Yes, sir. I'm sorry," Lowry mumbled. "I just wanted to help."

Mother gave him a hug and her eyes were kind. "I know, Lowry, but if you think about it, you wouldn't want to ride in a smothery old flour sack sideways on Old Sorrel, would you? Just remember, 'do unto others.' That's what we try to live by." She set down a trencher heaped with chicken pie and Lowry's mouth watered. "Son, you've done a man's work this evening. I'm proud of you." She handed him a spoon. "Here, tuck into this. I don't want you to go off without your supper, but hurry, please."

By the time he had finished his meal, everything was ready. Father led the way out back and fussed with hurried instructions. David swung up on Old Sorrel. The big horse's orangey-brown hide faded into the dusk, but the creamy mane and forelock reflected the lingering evening light.

Lowry loved Old Sorrel; together they had ripped out many a tree stump and plowed acres of fields, the horse's vast muscles rippling under the burnished coat. Big horses were usually clumsy and slow, but Old Sorrel possessed a surprising turn of speed. He had more personality than any other horse Lowry had ever known, to boot. Right now, he nosed David's foot as if to reassure the runaway, who jumped at each nighttime noise.

"God go with you, Lowry." Father waved, and they were off, across the woodlot and down the ravine to the creek bottom.

Before they had gone a mile, Lowry was so keyed up that when a dry twig cracked under Old Sorrel's hooves, it sounded like the report of a pistol. If Old Sorrel swiveled a lazy ear to catch a sound from behind, Lowry was sure that Luke Means was on his tail.

Despite Lowry's fears, they met no one. When they reached Mr. Hopkins's place, nestled in a secluded hollow five miles back of Ripley, Lowry leaned back to save his mount as they descended deep into the hollow. Lowry was a little scared of Arch Hopkins, who was a peculiar character. He kept to himself and ruled his place like a bantam rooster, but he was a master at training horses. The only time Lowry had been here before was when Father had traded for Old Sorrel.

"Who's there?" came a growl from the darkened front porch.

"Lowry Rankin, sir," he replied quickly. He knew if he hesitated to answer, he risked a round of buckshot.

"Come on." Mr. Hopkins hobbled painfully toward them; Lowry recalled that one hip had never mended properly after a nasty fall. As a result, Arch Hopkins never walked farther than across the yard. He rode his saddle mare, Bonny, everywhere else, and he rode her sidesaddle, like a lady, to spare his bad hip.

"Well, Old Sorrel, you remember your former master?" Mr. Hopkins grinned as the horse nuzzled his pockets. "My, we did a good job training you." He tickled the horse's soft ears, which tipped forward like a fox's, and kept up a murmured conversation. "You know what they say about you in town? Oh, yes, it's 'There are a great many good horses, but none is equal to Old Sorrel that carries the Rankin family.' Yessiree, it's a pity I let you go, old boy, but even you don't measure up to my sweet little dapple-gray, Bonny."

Lowry squirmed with impatience. "Mr. Hopkins, sir, this here's David. Father allowed you would know what to do for him. I'll be back for the other horse tomorrow mornin'." Funny, his accent, which he tried daily to shake, came back thicker than ever when he spoke with Mr. Hopkins, who was from Rockingham County, Virginia.

"Know what to do for him?" Mr. Hopkins repeated in amazement. "Man alive, I guess I do! I been a-takin' care of fugitives long before your pa ever took the notion. Now, y'all run along home, and don't push Old Sorrel, neither. Slow and steady saves wear and tear on his tendons. No racin', you hear, boy?" Mr. Hopkins shook a finger under Lowry's nose and motioned to David. "Come on into the house and Mrs. Hopkins will take care of y'all for a spell while I get my son John ready to take you on."

Just like that, Mr. Hopkins dismissed Lowry. It was plain to see that, to the Virginian, Lowry was just a child to be bossed. He slid down from the other horse's back and swung a leg over Old Sorrel. He would show Mr. Hopkins. He lifted the reins, ready to storm out of the yard at top speed.

"Wait a minute." The soft, dusky voice tethered Lowry like a rope until David appeared at his side. "Thank you, honey! Praise the Lord, I'se free, and ain't no one ever going to take me back to Mr. James no more. Maybe I'll find my family, too. You help' me like a man, and I'll—I'll never forget you," he choked.

All the hard knots of anger inside Lowry came untied. "I'll remember you, too, David," he promised solemnly. "God go with you." He turned for home.

All day Saturday, Ripley buzzed over David's escape. Everyone had a different opinion on just how Matthias James's slave made off right under his nose. Luke Means spread rumors that the Rankin family had something to do with the escape, but no one paid attention to him. As the days passed, it became obvious that David was gone for good. At the end of his fruitless search, Tice James himself came up with the explanation that amused townspeople the most.

"I swear, that runaway disappeared while I was looking at him, just as though he fell into a hole in the ground and pulled it in after him. Why," he lamented, "he must have taken an underground road." The younger Rankin children loved the story of how Tice's David escaped. Lowry smiled to think what they would say if they knew their brother had helped.

In the weeks that followed, Lowry had several more opportunities to aid fugitive slaves. Each time it was a welcome change from his usual responsibilities, and one that made him feel especially important. But no matter how much Lowry's life changed, the seasons still followed the pattern established before the beginning of time. By the end of May, the returning chimney swifts swirled like smoke over the chimneys of Ripley. At a signal no one but the swifts knew, the chittering flock spiraled down the chimney of an abandoned farmhouse. Lowry thought he would never grow tired of watching the birds' graceful flight.

As the summer deepened, the blackberry canes that Father cultivated bore a heavy yield of shiny, purple-black berries. Whenever Lowry popped a berry into his mouth, he could taste sunshine in them. Blackberries tasted good enough to make up for his purple-stained fingers, the briers that pierced his sleeves, the snakes that curled in the thickets, and the chiggers. Lowry scratched desperately at the chigger bites behind his knees until Mother slathered the red welts with lard. Later she made a luscious blackberry cobbler covered with a golden-brown latticework crust that oozed sugary purple juice, and everyone forgot about the inconveniences of blackberry picking.

July wound to a close, and early one morning as Lowry returned from transporting a fugitive, he watched a buck polish its fuzzy new antlers against an old tree stump until the velvet hung down in shreds. He managed a sleepy grin and thought about Spot, his pet of long ago. He rubbed his own chin hopefully, but he felt only downy peach fuzz.

Sometimes when Lowry took a load of firewood to town to hawk to the steamboats, he resented the steep path that dictated that he use sure-footed, slow oxen instead of speedier horses. Travel in Ripley could not be slower, but there were brighter days coming for Ohio. Father had read a late newspaper article that told of two amazing recent events in two cities. Both had taken place on the same day, the Fourth of July, 1828. On that date, John Quincy Adams, the nation's president, had broken ground at Little Falls, Maryland for the Chesapeake & Ohio Canal. During the festivities, the Marine Band played a special new song for the president, called "Hail to the Chief." Then a proud President Adams announced the canal's grand purpose. The C & O Canal would provide a trade route that canal boats could traverse, from the Appalachian Mountains to the Ohio River Valley. Lowry knew what a nuisance the little hill along Cornick's Run could be; he could not imagine trying to get over the craggy Appalachians with a wagon. A water route would be much easier and faster.

There was another interesting method of transportation in the news of July 4, 1828. Also on that date, Charles Carroll, the last living signer of the Declaration of Independence, broke ground in Baltimore, Maryland for the Baltimore & Ohio Railroad. The goal was to reach the Ohio River Valley for trade. Lowry did not know much about railroads or the engines that ran on them, but it sounded like an exciting race to Ohio. Which would reach the Ohio first, the canal or the railroad? How rich would the folks of Ripley become when there were two such easy ways of sending goods to the Eastern Seaboard?

That same year, there was word of another way to get rich. In Dahlonega, Georgia, gold had been discovered on Cherokee Indian land. Dahlonega meant "precious yellow metal" in the Cherokee language. The discovery had little practical value, however, except to the Cherokee nation, because the gold was on their ancestral land. Nevertheless, Lowry wished he had just one gold nugget to spend as he liked.

The year wore on toward fall and Father grew increasingly agitated as he read the newspaper. It was an election year and President Adams, the incumbent, and his challenger, General Andrew Jackson, regularly dragged each other's names through the mud in the nastiest campaign yet seen. The Democratic Republicans touted their candidate, Jackson, with smoky barbecues, pompous tree plantings, and one bunting-festooned parade after another. Jackson supporters allowed that John Quincy Adams had only won the presidency because of a corrupt bargain with Henry Clay, Kentucky's favorite son. Clay was no favorite of Father's, Lowry knew. He supposed that Father would vote for Jackson, fondly called Old Hickory.

President Adams's cronies, members of the National Republicans, accused Jackson of being a violent ruffian, a man who was ready to duel to the death at the drop of a hat. He certainly had a mind of his own, as evidenced by his performance in the Seminole War of 1818. Rather than allow Great Britain to incite the Indians to harass white settlers in Florida after the War of 1812, Jackson waged a one-man campaign to drive all the Indians out of the Southeast. Thus, he generated a lot of criticism about his character and his unpredictability. Some of his detractors even alleged that he was of mixed race. Lowry knew that you might as well put down one vote for Jackson if you used that kind of argument with Father.

When November rolled around, Andrew Jackson won the election in a landslide on Lowry's twelfth birthday, but it took a spell for the news to travel to Ripley. A general celebration followed. Right through Jackson's inauguration in March of 1829, there was plenty of crowing in Ripley that the Era of the Common Man had arrived.

In early spring, Lowry plowed the cornfield with a team of oxen hitched to a moldboard plow. He did not have twelve yoke of oxen like Elisha in the first book of Kings, but Lowry knew that his wooden plow with the polished metal plowshare was much the same. Still, he could plow an acre in about twenty-four hours, a big improvement over the ninety-six hours per acre that his ancestors spent preparing the soil with just a hoe. He watched the earth scour from the moldboard in neat rolls that covered last year's stubble and this year's weeds. Occasionally, the thick clay base would stick to the moldboard, and then Lowry would have to scrape it off with his paddle staff, a sort of long-handled spade. Soon he clutched the handles again and shouted "Giddap!" The chains rattled, the plow creaked, and the oxen lumbered forward for another pass over the field.

Lowry was glad he could stumble along behind the oxen in a daze, because a party of fugitives had passed through the night before, and he was dog-tired. Because there were several people in this group, Lowry's younger brother, David, had ridden along for the first time. Lowry had never been so grateful for company. With David along, time had passed much faster on the long ride home from the back of beyond. Alas, David was worn out, and Father had allowed him to sleep late this morning, almost until the old rooster crowed at sunup.

When the plowing was done, the Rankin family waited anxiously for the oak leaves to be as large as a squirrel's ear. That was when the leaves first came out, and Lowry had to look close to see them behind all the pollen tassels. By the time the leaves were squirrel-ear sized, he knew it was warm enough to plant corn. The earlier the seed went into the ground, Lowry knew, the better the yield, and a good yield was vital because the Rankin family continued to grow. Now the family included Ibby, David, Calvin, Samuel, Julia, Johnny, and Andrew, all younger than Lowry, the big brother. At suppertime, the Rankins made quite a crowd around the table.

Lowry tried to remember how important corn planting was as he worked. He was glad he had cross-checked the field with a double-runner sled. When the horses dragged it long-ways, the sled had made neat rows about forty inches apart, because of the runners. Then Lowry had guided the sled across the field so new rows crossed the others at right angles. Now there was a neat grid in the earth, and the Rankin children planted corn at each crossing. After planting, they would tend the corn three times. When it came time to weed, half-hill, or hill the corn, there were straight rows to walk. Then, with a flip of the hoe, Lowry and his brothers could either cover weeds or mound soil around the corn-stalks. The extra soil helped the young plants withstand hard rains and high winds.

He was getting ahead of himself, to think about cultivating before they had even planted any corn. He watched Ibby's thin back as she trudged ahead of him. Lowry knew his sister was hot, for the back of her dress and her sunbonnet were damp. He knew she was tired, too, because there were dark smudges under her eyes, and she yawned a lot. Ibby's job in the family business was to feed the fugitives. Mother was usually busy with the newest baby and needed to rest when she could. There was no rest for Lowry and Ibby, though, because the corn must be planted if they wanted to eat. His sister poked a hole with a long, pointed dibble stick at the crosshatch in the soil, and then she reached into the pouch slung over her shoulder. He heard her sing the rhyme they had known ever since they were small as she dropped five golden kernels into each hole:

One for the blackbird,
One for the crow,
One for the cutworm,
And two to grow.

Behind Ibby, Lowry hoed about an inch and a half of soil over the kernels, and tamped it lightly with the back of the hoe. Even though he could see his breath this morning, sweat rolled off the tip of his nose, but there was no time to wipe his face. His shoes slid over the mellowed earth and he followed Ibby all day as they planted corn.

Planting season and growing season waned into the bountiful harvest. The talk in Ripley now was about David Walker, a free black man who lived in Boston, Massachusetts. He had issued a strident appeal that slavery should be abolished and that the freedmen should then be treated with the same respect as white men. Father's sermons, always inspiring, waxed eloquent in his support for such a cause.

Lowry looked deep in his own heart and decided to make a public profession, by joining the church, of what he had known for some time now—that he followed Jesus Christ, the One who was no respecter of persons. He thought Father and Mother would bust, they were so happy. Father gravely reminded Lowry that he must come before the elders of the church and have his faith examined, but Lowry felt he was ready.

He would never forget the—was it right to say *contempt?*—he saw in the six elders' solemn faces when he came for his examination. They all felt Lowry was too young to make such a decision, but Father reminded the church officers that his eldest son had just turned thirteen, and that the Lord Jesus himself had taught in the temple when he was only twelve. The examination began, but Lowry never wanted to be in that situation again. Oh, he answered the questions all right, though his indignation grew as the elders failed to hide their skepticism about his commitment.

Finally Father brought a halt to the proceedings and pointed out that Lowry had answered far more questions than the average adult who wished to join the church, and answered them well. He said to either let Lowry become a member, or reject him, but the questioning must end. Gruffly, the elders invited Lowry to join the church, but now his stubbornness flared. He was tired of school, tired of church, tired of transporting slaves, tired of anything that adults commanded him to do, as if he could not think for himself. The minutes ticked past while he considered. Did he really want to be a member of a church that felt he was not old enough to know his own mind?

In the end he decided to join, but it was days before his resentment over the cool treatment died. As time passed, he wondered whether there had been any bitterness over Father's support of David Walker's stand, but he doubted that church elders would peevishly hold an adult's opinions against his own son. Well, Lowry had done his best; he had revealed what was in his heart. What happened from now on was in the hands of the Lord.

Chapter 5

As the new year of 1830 dawned, residents of the Kentucky towns along the Ohio River could hardly contain their joy. Almost three years earlier, surveying had begun for an ambitious project—the Maysville Road, a macadamized road to be built from Maysville, Kentucky, just upriver from Ripley, to Lexington, over sixty miles away. Lowry read in the paper that the Maysville Road would eventually pass Carlisle, the Kentucky town where he had known such happy times—before Sherwood's whipping. The Maysville and Lexington Turnpike Road Company had been formed to collect subscriptions to finance the road, which would open yet another trade route to bring wealth and commerce to Kentucky.

Statesman Henry Clay was a great champion of the Maysville Road. Farmers like the Rankins supported it, too, just as they supported the work on the canal and railroad that were inching toward the Ohio River Valley. Lately, the people had decided to solicit federal aid for the Maysville Road, just as the builders of the canal and railroad projects had received, and the Maysville Road Bill was drafted. If the bill passed, the government would have the right to assist in building state and local roads by taking shares of stock in local turnpike companies, such as the Maysville & Lexington Company.

One year into his administration, President Andrew Jackson already had many foes in Ohio. To reduce the United States' debt, Jackson had refused to grant federal funds to states for railroads or canals, the very things Ohio needed to aid its growth in commerce. Matters were downright ugly in Jackson's own Cabinet. Vice President John C. Calhoun had, as a former secretary of war, recommended that Jackson be censured, or officially criticized, for his role in the Seminole War of 1818. When Jackson found out, he made Calhoun his sworn enemy. For his part, Calhoun almost openly defied the president at the Jefferson Day Banquet on April 30. Jackson flung down a gauntlet with his toast, "Our Federal Union: it must be preserved." Calhoun, a South Carolinian to the core, responded with his own icy toast: "The Union: next to our Liberty, most dear." Many people wondered whether Jackson would hold out an olive branch to another bitter enemy, Henry Clay, by urging passage of the Maysville Road Bill.

Lowry could not remember the Kentucky landowners ever being more genial when they came across the river to Ripley. Even Ohio transplant Thomas McCague's eyes gleamed with pride when he spoke of the Maysville Road Bill. Lowry cheered when Ripley got the news that the bill had passed in the House of Representatives on April 29, 1830. By May 15, the Senate had passed the bill. Now all that remained was a mere formality, the moment when Old Hickory, the president of the common man, would sign the bill into law.

By early June, the name of the Maysville Road was on the lips of every American; it had gained national fame. If only the fame had come for a different reason! For on May 27, 1830, Andrew Jackson had vetoed the bill because the Maysville Road fell entirely within the state of Kentucky. He maintained his stand not to commit federal funds for state projects.

At first, Kentuckians were shocked and mortified, then bitter. In a defiant mood, they completed the first section of the Maysville Road, a four-mile stretch from the hill back of Maysville over to Washington, Kentucky, by November of 1830. It was the first macadamized road in the commonwealth of Kentucky, and folks along the river were justifiably proud. Beneath the surface, however, resentment burned. It was rumored that Jackson had vetoed the bill because of Henry Clay's connection with it, and it was common knowledge that Jackson loathed Clay.

The mood changed from support for the president to defiance. The popular ditty of the Jackson campaign, "The Hunters of Kentucky," became a sort of warning when Kentucky men sang it now:

We are a hardy free-born race, each man to fear a stranger,
Whate'er the game we join in chase, despising toil and danger;
And if a daring foe annoys, whate'er his strength and forces,
We'll show him that Kentucky boys are alligator horses.
Oh, Kentucky! the hunters of Kentucky.

Lowry privately changed the last line to, "Oh, Kentucky! The slave hunters of Kentucky!" Father wondered if the Kentuckians would break with Andrew Jackson over his slight of their state. If that happened, he said, their support for Calhoun, the slave owner and supporter of state's rights, would not be far behind.

School started again in October, and to Lowry's great disgust, he and David were in attendance every day that school was in session. That fall, Lowry began to think about his life's vocation. He knew the day would soon come when he would be expected to start earning his keep by bringing in an income. Father's salary had shrunk from five hundred dollars a year when he began as a minister to just three hundred and fifty dollars. Counting the twelve members of his own family, now that baby Mary was here, the fugitives who stopped through, the hired help, and the occasional aunt, uncle, or cousin who came to visit, Lowry could not see how they all survived on what the church paid Father, yet there was always enough. Lowry knew that Father had never been in the ministry for the money, anyway. No, abolition was what drove Father. He saw it as his mission to do everything in his power under God to secure an end to slavery.

When he considered a vocation, Lowry always thought back to his informal printing apprenticeship with Mr. Ammen, the Rankins' neighbor down in Ripley. With Lowry's help, the editor had printed a thousand copies of Father's anti-slavery letters, the ones he'd originally written to his brother Thomas. Half of the books were bound, at a cost of eighty dollars, which Father paid by releasing Mr. Ammen from a few months' rent. The other half were stored unbound in a warehouse in Maysville—at least they were until someone burned the warehouse to the ground. Every remaining copy of Father's book was lost, and no one had ever been charged with the crime.

Just after the first of the year, 1831, a miracle occurred. One of the five hundred bound copies that had been distributed locally found its way into the hands of a Quaker gentleman back east, who wrote to ask Father's permission for a friend to reprint the letters in his anti-slavery publication, *The Liberator*. William Lloyd Garrison was the publisher's name, and he lived in Boston. Of course, Father willingly agreed—anything to advance the cause of abolition—and soon his persuasive letters were back in circulation. But Father did not receive a dime in compensation.

The thread that stitched 1831 together for Lowry was the steady stream of refugees—desperate men, women, and sometimes children—who escaped from Kentucky plantation holders and came to the red brick house on the hill overlooking Ripley, Ohio, as regular as clockwork. The Rankins did not keep a written record of how many runaways passed through—it would not be safe—but as near as Lowry could figure, at least one or more fugitives came up the hill in search of freedom every week.

Father saw to it that the farm work continued uninterrupted. Not only did the family need the food for their table, as well as the small cash income they could earn by selling their surplus goods in town, but the regular commerce of the farm kept them actively involved in the life of the community. It was important that no one suspect the Rankins' role in the escapes.

In the fall of 1831, Lowry began classes at Ripley College. There he was with older boys, many from out of state. He still sang every Sunday morning in the church choir, too, even though his voice cracked and slid up the scale alarmingly these days. Gradually, his peach fuzz thickened into some genuine whiskers and he learned to shave. He did not think he would ever follow the fashion and wear a beard; in that respect, he was like Father. To his chagrin, Lowry did not grow much taller, but he did notice that he grew stronger. All those long days of hard work and long nights of riding were good for something, he supposed. His eyes were often red-rimmed, but nobody ever asked him about it.

One Sunday morning in November found the Rankin family in church, just like always. Every week they attended the early service, Sunday school, and second service, and then went home with someone in town for the midday meal. Typically, they lingered with friends until the service at early candlelight. After supper in the evening, Father led family worship at home, just as he did every night. Sunday was a day dedicated to worshipping the Lord.

"Good morning, Lowry."

Lowry's head snapped up. That sounded like Amanda Kephart. His face burned hotter than fire and he peeked over his shoulder. Sure enough, there she sat with her family in the pew behind the Rankins. He goggled at her, unable to say a word.

"You don't have to talk. I know you're bashful. I just thought I'd say hello before church starts." Amanda stared down at her hymnal and her long black lashes veiled her cornflower-blue eyes.

Lowry managed a weak grin and slid down in the pew. Confound it, why did he have to act like a sick calf when Amanda was around? Of course, Ibby, David, and Calvin did not help matters as they snickered behind their hands at him.

One look from Mother wiped the grin from Lowry's face. The scolding he had gotten for not speaking in school was fresh in his mind. Mr. Brockway had spoken to Mother again just yesterday, and she had come home with fire in her eyes.

"Lowry, I will not have it. You will speak when you are spoken to, and you will stop this shy foolishness. If I hear tell of it again, you're going to have a dose of 'peach tree tea.'" That was Mother's name for a whipping. She often threatened to cut a peach switch from the orchard, but all the children knew it was an empty threat. She did not have time to hunt for a switch.

Now Mother glared at Lowry and jerked her head toward Amanda. The church organ burst into great swells of music that drowned out all conversation, but that did not stop Mother. "Say howdy," she mouthed.

He was sure he would never live through it. He swallowed hard and straightened. Then he looked back at Amanda. "Howdy, Amanda," he barely whispered, but somehow she heard him. Her eyes sparkled and her rosy lips turned up in a smile.

His heart hammered against his ribs, but he had done it. He had spoken to her for the first time. Amanda liked it, too, he could see that. Maybe Mother was right. Maybe there was something to this "howdy" idea of hers. The opening hymn passed in a happy blur. Afterwards, Lowry could not have said what the hymn was, but he did notice that Amanda sang it clear and sweet, like a meadowlark.

The good feeling carried over as he filed up to sing with the choir and then listened to Father's sermon. He suddenly longed to be part of the service. It felt right to be here among people who loved God as he did. For the barest instant, he envied Father, who had known from the time he was seven years old that he would be a minister.

Lowry explored the notion a little more. What would it be like to stand up there in front of a congregation and talk about

Jesus? Maybe, if he had somebody like Amanda to help him—but what was he thinking? He gave himself a mental shake and concentrated on the message. Father was drawing on an old standard, "And ye shall know the truth, and the truth shall make you free." How hard could preaching be if you used the same sermons over and over again? Nevertheless, he paid strict attention for the rest of the service.

Monday morning, instead of poking along Cornick's Run to school, Lowry skidded down the steep ridge of crumbly clay that led directly to town, almost to the church's front door. The school was just a bit further on. He could see some merit in Father's suggestion that they build stone steps down the slope to town, although it would be backbreaking work. They would have to notch the clay, lay some flat stones, then anchor smooth, long slabs overtop of those to make steps, but he sure would have an easier time getting to school. It seemed like a lot of work, though, just for the family, because no one else ever came up that way. Visitors from town used the bridle path along Cornick's Run.

Goodness knows, our house is always full to bursting with visitors, Lowry mused. Right now, Benjamin Templeton, a free black college student, boarded with the Rankins while he attended Ripley College.

Most of Ripley did not care one way or the other whether Ben Templeton attended Ripley College. It was no skin off their noses if the black boy wanted to be a minister. However, Lowry had heard rumors of one man who seethed with rage at the mention of Templeton, and that was Luke Means's big brother, Zeke. Despite Luke's dismal showing in school thus far, Zeke tried to get his baby brother admitted to Ripley College with the other two hundred and fifty students. He paid five dollars and promised to scrape together the rest of the ten-dollar tuition soon. It was an empty promise, however, and Mr. Nate Brockway, Lowry's old schoolmaster and now the president of Ripley College, expelled Luke.

It was common knowledge that Zeke exploded into ugly threats at any mention of Ben Templeton. The story went that President Brockway had even received a threatening note, which said, "As my brother is too poor to go to your college, a colored boy shall not. Turn him out, or I will cowhide him in the street." The college board refused to be intimidated. Instead, Templeton continued going to school every day, but always in the company of President Brockway or Professor Simpson.

That had been a month ago. Nothing had come of the threats, so Ben was allowed to walk to school unattended again. Lowry had hung around this morning, waiting to see if Ben wanted to walk down the hill with him, but the good-natured young man had declined.

Just before noon, Lowry sat on the hard slab bench in the schoolroom and thought dreamily of Amanda Kephart. The schoolmaster read out a sum to be copied on the slates, and he wrote it down mechanically. His stomach rumbled and he hunched over to stop it. When the class had solved the problem, the teacher said they might take their lunch pails outside, for the autumn day was unusually mellow and warm. Lowry resolved to take his nooning with Amanda; he would meet her as she came out of the old schoolhouse. As he stepped out the doorway, he saw Ben Templeton heading toward home for dinner, a precaution that Father had urged. The only thing on Lowry's mind right now was his own dinner with Amanda, but what happened next changed everything.

Zeke Means stepped out of an alleyway and blocked Ben Templeton's way. Lowry saw a hefty whip in Zeke's beefy hand. He tasted acid at the back of his throat as the cowhide's leaded tips whistled through the air and slashed Ben's legs. "No!" he screamed, and all the horror of Sherwood's beating, so long suppressed, flooded back. A stark memory of the scarlet beads of blood that had welled up from his friend's flayed golden skin brought tears to his eyes. He had to *do* something. He flung down his dinner pail and ran toward Zeke.

Before Lowry was halfway across the road, Zeke managed several brutal strokes. Then everything happened at once. Thomas McCague appeared out of nowhere, seized the whip, and wrestled it from Zeke's hand. President Brockway shoved Zeke to the ground. Zeke grunted as more bodies piled on to hold him until the law arrived. He did not seem to care. He lay there with his face pressed in the mud and smiled to hear the men shout and women sobbing. Father emerged from the crowd, his face distorted and terrible. Lowry saw Zeke roll his eyes as Father wept and helped Ben stand. Ben trembled, the pain and fear altering his countenance so much that Lowry hardly recognized him.

The constable yanked Zeke to his feet. "What do you have to say for yourself?" he demanded.

"I don't need to say nothin'," Zeke growled. "I done said it all. If my brother can't go to this college, no slave boy's going to. It don't make no difference that he wants to be a minister and my brother is the son of a tavern keeper." Hate screwed up his face and he spat in the direction of Father and Ben Templeton. "There's what I think of ministers!" He screamed hoarsely now and his rage spilled over at Father. "Don't you come visit our house no more. We don't need to hear no gospel. You come next week, like you been coming, and I'll blast your britches full of buckshot."

Instinctively Lowry moved to Father's side, and the movement attracted Zeke's attention. "*You!*" He pointed at Lowry. "You're the cause of it all." Lowry flinched. Zeke shouted, "My brother would still be in school right now if it wasn't for you picking a fight with him. Oh, yes, he done told me all about it. I bet you wanna be a minister, too. Well, first off, you better learn to talk. But even if you do, ain't nobody in Ripley gives a dern what you have to say." Then the constable wrenched Zeke's arm behind him and escorted him away.

Lowry stared at the ground and wished the earth would open up and swallow him whole. He knew Zeke was right. No one cared what he had to say.

"Let's get Ben to Dr. Campbell's, Nate." Father spoke to Mr. Brockway and his voice seemed to come from a long way off. "Pay Zeke no mind, son," he consoled half-heartedly as he hovered over Ben Templeton. He did not look at Lowry.

"I won't, Father," he replied, but no one heard him and that stung like a whip.

"Don't listen to Zeke, Lowry." The voice came from behind him, and he knew it was Amanda. He shuffled his feet and angrily knuckled away a tear. "I fetched your dinner pail. Let's eat. I'm hungry, aren't you?" she coaxed. He shrugged his shoulders and shook his head. From the corner of his eye he saw the strained look on the girl's face and despised himself.

She was not a quitter, though, and gave it one more try. "I think you would make a fine preacher, Lowry, if that's what you want to be." He heard a curious note in her voice, almost like she was crying, but he did not meet her eyes. The next time he looked up, she was gone.

Chapter 6

LOWRY TOLD HIMSELF THAT he was glad he had not let Amanda rescue him. He had tried to *do* something to help Ben Templeton. Other people better suited to the task had gotten there first. Well, Lowry had learned his lesson; after his public humiliation at the hands of Zeke Means, he knew beyond a shadow of a doubt that he would never be a minister. The best course was to quit school and take up a trade. He planned to ask Father about it right away. *That is, if Father is not too busy caring for Ben Templeton,* he thought bitterly.

After Ben's terrifying experience, Father tutored him at home. Late in December, Lowry worked up the courage to approach Father about quitting school. Father, who had been Lowry's staunch champion when he joined the church, now used the same argument the elders had advanced against him.

"Absolutely not, Lowry, it is out of the question. You're not old enough to make such a decision."

Lowry's jaw dropped. "You said I was old enough to know that I wanted to join the church, and I was only thirteen then. I'm fifteen now!"

"Choosing a profession is different. Besides, you are going to enter the ministry. We desperately need more ministers who support abolition."

"But, Father! I don't want to be a minister. I could never speak before a crowd, and no one would listen to me, anyway. I want to be a carpenter." The more agitated Lowry became, the more his chest tightened. He wondered what had happened to the air that he could not draw enough for a deep breath.

Father was adamant. "Nonsense! You are much too smart to fritter away your life at a common trade."

"A common trade! You are proud enough of what you can do with your hands! How many times have you told me that you made your own wedding shoes?" Lowry waved his arms. "You built this house! I watched you do it! Now I want to build things."

Father watched him thoughtfully, and Lowry held his peace. A new light came into Father's eyes then; patience was etched into his face, just like when he tried to back a balky colt between the shafts of a buggy.

"Well, well, Lowry, we won't argue. Why don't you stick out this school year and give your idea some serious thought?" The words sounded like a suggestion, but Father's word was law. Lowry stormed out into the frigid December air to attack the woodpile. As he split the wood, he thought about the old adage that firewood warms you twice, once when you cut it and once when you burn it. He was hotter than blazes before he resigned himself to another weary year of farm work, school work, and transporting refugees.

Once in a great while during 1832, Lowry had a chance to relax. When raccoons threatened to make a shambles of his carefully planted corn, Lowry and his cousins staged a coon hunt for the next full moon. The Rankin hounds, especially Cutie, entered wholeheartedly into the pursuit. When Cutie treed a raccoon, all Ripley knew it, for her baying echoed through the hollows. By the end of the evening, the corn on Rankin's hill was safe for a while, thanks to some tired but happy boys.

Lowry savored a particularly sweltering afternoon late in August when the boys from school all gathered at the covered bridge and warned the girls to stay away. One of the locals, who would remain nameless if anyone were questioned, kicked out a board from the side of the covered bridge, right over the middle of the creek, and soon a steady parade of buck naked boys were jumping into the cold, rushing creek below. That removing the board was an act of vandalism, nobody seemed to consider. All Lowry knew was that he had toiled under the fiery sun until he was caked with sweat and dust, and it was heavenly to plunge into the icy depths of the creek. A covered bridge made a private place to sneak a kiss from a pretty girl, too—the boys even called them kissing bridges. Lowry pondered this thought as he paddled blissfully upstream to jump in again.

What he thought about most that summer, though, was his argument for quitting school. Some days, he imagined brilliant speeches that would cut Father's arguments down cold. After all, Uncle William McNishie, an architect and carpenter, had proposed that Lowry might live with them as a drafting apprentice. Uncle William and Aunt Lucinda, one of Mother's sisters, lived in the Rankins' old apartment on Front Street. Even with this ideal arrangement, there were days when Lowry could not think of the simplest reason that he should take up carpentry.

In the end, however, Lowry got his wish to avoid school, though not for the reasons he had devised. There was no school for him or anyone else that fall. Every business in Ripley closed, and there were no church services or public gatherings of any kind. For weeks, everyone in town forgot about everything but the Asiatic cholera epidemic that began in the fall of 1832.

An infected passenger had disembarked from a steamer at Ripley, and that was all it took to spread the deadly disease. For days, Dr. Campbell relied upon Father and Mother to help care for more than one hundred and fifty ill friends and neighbors. By the grace of God, none of the Rankins came down with cholera, from Father all the way down to Lowry's days-old new baby brother, William.

Lowry often helped Dr. Campbell when Mother needed to

care for baby William, and thus he was plunged into the world of medicine. Dr. Campbell's resources were painfully limited. Sometimes he soothed a fever with cold water applied to the patient's head and face; sometimes a tepid bath worked wonders. The doctor used ipecacuanha to induce vomiting, and calomel to keep folks' bowels flowing freely. His last resort was bloodletting. Dr. Campbell did not hold much faith in this ancient treatment, however. He explained to Lowry, his unwilling assistant, that a cholera patient's blood pressure was already dangerously low. In fact, Dr. Campbell despaired that he had no real recourse against any of the symptoms of cholera. Diarrhea, vomiting, fever, plummeting blood pressure, and a thready pulse—the old dependable remedies only made them worse.

So the disease ran its course, in anywhere from a few hours to a full week, unchecked except by the mercy of the Lord. Although Dr. Campbell tended the sick around the clock, about four people died every day. The stillness of death hung over the town. The president of Ripley College, Mr. Brockway, was the first to go, in only a matter of hours.

One casualty in particular broke Lowry's heart. Mr. Kephart, the hotelkeeper, had let a room to the original infected passenger. Within hours, Amanda's father had suffered excruciating pain and succumbed to the cholera with a swiftness that stunned Lowry. He would never forget Amanda's face at her father's burial, where Father officiated briefly. Her bewildered grief stabbed at Lowry's heart. He agonized over how he had rebuffed her support after Ben Templeton's beating. Now her father was dead, and her little brother Billy was very ill. A horrible thought numbed Lowry—what if Amanda died? He prayed fervently that Billy would recover, and that Amanda would be spared. When word of Billy Kephart's slow convalescence circulated, Lowry was the first one at the door to tell Amanda how glad he was. Billy's recovery gave Ripley hope that the epidemic had peaked.

There came a day when the cholera deaths ended. A blessed routine filled the sad days again, and gradually smiles returned to the faces of dear friends and loved ones who had survived the epidemic.

Just before supper on the eve of Lowry's sixteenth birthday, he and Father sat on the back porch and watched a slow snowfall drifting down like white smoke. Father cleared his throat. "Well, Lowry, school starts tomorrow."

"Yes, sir."

"Have you come to a decision?"

Lowry considered; he had waited for this moment for a long time. He geared himself up to begin, but Father said, "Son, I—stay home tomorrow." The silence stretched between them until they could hear the snowflakes swish across the porch.

Father passed a hand across his eyes. "I am so tired. It seems like all the fight has gone out from me. When I think of your mother, and all she has been through with the new baby, and all the sickness, and our friends," he continued brokenly, "stay home."

Lowry stared at his father as if he had never really seen him before. He noticed the fine lines at the corners of Father's eyes, the gray streaks in his dark hair. For the first time in Lowry's life, Father seemed very vulnerable. His words seemed to come from far away.

"There was a time, Lowry, when I thought you would be a minister, like me. But if that call hasn't come from God, then there is no call. For a while, I thought you might practice medicine, but now . . ." Father's eyes were bleak. "That is a profession I would wish on no one. Help me with the plowing, come spring, and then you are free to learn carpentry with your Uncle McNishie. I know he is a fine Christian man," he continued, "so I give my consent on two conditions. First, maintain your Christian integrity if you meet workmen who do not share your high moral standards. Second, finish at Ripley College when you serve out your apprenticeship.

And there is one other thing. I want you to come home on Saturday nights and go to church with us on Sundays, just as you always have."

Just like that, Lowry marveled, he had won. He could not put his gratitude into words, but he squeezed Father's shoulder.

"Supper's ready," Mother called. The two men stood up together. Father deferred, so Lowry crossed first to the low bench where a tin basin rested. He tipped some water into it from the bucket and took up the slab of lye soap. He washed his hands and dried them on the clean feed sack towel that hung stiffly on a nail. Father followed suit, and together they went in for supper.

Late that next April, Lowry plowed his last acre behind Old Sorrel. The big horse, who was literally as strong as an ox, had saved Lowry from many a tight place over the years. Together, Lowry and his strapping comrade had struggled to break sod in a new field by day and often transported three fugitives at once on the horse's broad back on the same night. Lowry brushed away a sentimental tear as he hugged Old Sorrel's neck.

The next morning, Lowry rode into town with David. "Here's your trunk." David hoisted the wooden chest from the wagon bed and swung it to the ground beside Uncle William McNishie's front steps in Ripley.

"Thanks." Lowry hung his head; he had no idea how to say good-bye.

David grinned slyly and thrust out his hand to shake. Lowry's brother was thirteen now, and he was at Lowry's side every time a fugitive needed transport. He knew better than anyone except Lowry the sacrifices that the "family business" required. Lowry wished he had his younger brother's philosophical nature to help take the adversity in stride. David had teased Lowry for days about his upcoming "vacation" from farm work, and now he was at it again. "Maybe it won't be so much of a vacation, after all. I hear the youngest apprentice has to do all the dirty work. You'll soon take up preaching."

"Never in a million years. You know I would rather be a mechanic," Lowry protested. "Uncle William will teach me architectural drafting and all forms of trussing. It won't be long until he sees how good I am."

"I know you will be a fine draftsman. I was only joshing. You have always liked working with your hands." David's eyes twinkled. "Still, you know Father says we need more abolition ministers. He might have let you choose, but I think he halfway believes you will still preach abolition."

There was that word, the one that had haunted Lowry all his life. Abolition had forced him to leave his boyhood paradise in Kentucky. Abolition had caused him to fight with Luke Means on his first day of school in Ripley, when the bully had insulted Mother. Abolition caused him to lose sleep at night when he escorted runaways, and abolition caused him to remain in school long after he wanted to leave.

Before he knew what he was doing, Lowry grabbed David's sleeve and dragged him into a deserted alley.

"Abolition!" The spiteful word exploded like a charge of gunpowder. "Always abolition! Are slaves more important than Father's own sons?" Lowry's conscience pricked and he thought of his friend Sherwood. He shook it off. "Father wakes us up in the wee hours of the morning, and we saddle horses to ride five, ten, fifteen, twenty miles, *all night* to the next station," he hissed. "Then we hustle home before dawn, snatch an hour of sleep if we're lucky, and wake up to milk cows and chop wood, and then off we trot to school, where we can barely stay awake to learn our lessons," Lowry finished bitterly. The world came back into sharp focus and he saw David's stunned expression.

“Lowry, you don’t mean that!” David whispered miserably. “We are doing God’s work when we carry slaves to freedom. Surely you believe that!”

Lowry’s dander was up now, and he would not back down. “We may be doing God’s work, but we’re doing it Father’s way. That’s what I believe,” Lowry scoffed. “He wants me to be a minister. A *minister*, when I’m too shy to even speak in school! I’ll never be a minister. No one wants to hear what I have to say, anyway. I don’t hold with slavery, but I don’t feel called to preach against it, either. I just want to keep as far away from it as possible.” A powerful image of Sherwood, unconscious and bleeding, burned into Lowry’s mind, but again he quenched his conscience. “I sure won’t stand before a congregation to speak my mind about abolition. *I am too shy*. I want to build things with my hands, not preach to people,” he said. “People just make fun of the way I talk.” He stopped in confusion. He had finally said it aloud.

“So that’s it.” David’s voice held a note of discovery. He walked slowly back to Lowry’s trunk.

Lowry shook his head and changed his tack, embarrassed that he had revealed too much of himself. He followed David and plucked at his sleeve. “Please listen to me, David. You love farm work. You can’t wait to take a flatboat loaded with your own goods down to New Orleans. You want to marry and have a family, and to live off the land. Try to understand. How would you feel if Father said you should be a preacher instead?” Lowry pleaded.

His brother ignored him. “I think I do understand, now. The reason you didn’t talk in school is because Luke Means thrashed you on your first day. He made fun of the way you talk. That’s it, isn’t it?” David accused. “You’re not shy at all.”

Lowry tightened the leather straps on the trunk. “I’m tellin’ you one thing right now, I ain’t a-gonna be a preacher.” His accent always came back thickest when he was upset, but he hardly noticed. His eyes smarted; he and David had shared so much. What a terrible way to leave his brother!

As if David knew what Lowry was thinking, he begged, "Don't go off like this. I'm sorry. Please don't be angry with me."

Lowry's scowl evaporated like mist in the sun. He hugged his younger brother. "I'm the one who's sorry. Forgive me." He made a lame attempt at humor. "Maybe I won't do well at drafting. Perhaps I may just change my mind and become a minister after all," he joked feebly, but he knew in his heart that no one in the world could persuade him to go into the ministry.

David smiled with relief and slapped Lowry's back as he left. "No, you're sixteen, old enough to know your own mind. You'll be a carpenter for the rest of your days."

The summer flew by as Lowry settled quickly into his new life. He loved learning carpentry. The men in Uncle William's shop were friendly, and Lowry saw Father nearly every day because he was building a new church house in Ripley. Sometimes Uncle William and Lowry even helped Father, when business was slow. Lowry had even grown to love living in town again, partly because he could see Amanda whenever he was free.

In August, Mother stopped by Uncle William's with several bushels of peaches from the Rankin orchard. She told Lowry to take a few bushels to the Kepharts, too. A few days later, Lowry helped Amanda dry the peaches for winter storage. Together they pared peaches, and the slippery peels littered the cool front porch despite Lowry's best efforts. They put the skinned peaches into a pan of water to keep them from browning. Amanda set a quart of water to boil, then added about a pound of sugar. She stirred while Lowry lugged the pans of peaches to the kitchen, which was already crammed to bursting with fat glasses of pickles and everything that went into them.

Lowry carefully added the whole peaches to the thin syrup. As the syrup boiled around the ripe fruit, thick bubbles popped and released fragrant steam until the whole kitchen smelled like sugary peach juice. Amanda watched carefully until the peaches looked translucent. She let them cool a little, split and stoned them with a sharp knife, then set them to boil again until they were very tender. Then she took them up to drain and made another, thicker syrup with another pound of sugar.

"It has to boil down almost to a candy," she said as she fussed over the pot. Lowry lounged at the table behind her and admired Amanda's back as she stirred. Her pink calico was sprigged with rosebuds, and a crisp white muslin fichu hung to a point between her shoulders. The apron strings curved almost to the floor beneath the neat bow; maybe it was her mother's apron, he reflected. *My, it is hotter than fire here in the kitchen.* Amanda must have felt the same way, for just then she wiped her forehead with the back of her free hand.

Afterward, Lowry could not remember exactly what happened next. He heard a loud pop and a cry of pain from Amanda. She nursed her hand as tears welled up in her eyes.

"What happened, Mandy? Did you burn yourself?" Lowry was up in an instant. He reached for the jug of apple cider vinegar next to the pickle jars and sloshed some on a rag. "Let me see." He took her reddened hand gently and held the dampened rag to the burn.

"Why, it hardly hurts at all," she marveled after a moment. "Thank you." She lowered her eyes, and he realized he was still holding her hand.

"You're welcome." He did not let go, and to his delight, she did not try to pull away. A faint tinge of pink spread across her cheeks and she looked at him. Her hand felt soft and warm. He looked into her eyes and wondered why he had ever thought they were the faded blue of cornflowers. They were more like a deep blue September sky. Then he could think of nothing else except how much he wanted to kiss her. He leaned closer, so close that his breath ruffled a golden wisp of her hair.

"Hey, Low-ry!"

He dropped Amanda's hand like a hot potato and dabbed it with the rag as her younger brother Billy raced into the kitchen. "Did you bring my sailboat? You promised to bring one for me, next time you came." His peaked face sent a stab of pain through Lowry's heart; he could not be angry. The younger boy wrinkled his nose suddenly. "Phew, what stinks? Mandy, you smell like pickles!"

Amanda laughed fondly and smoothed his hair. "Oh, Billy!" She held up her red hand. "See, I burned myself. Lowry said that vinegar would take away the sting, and it has. My hand feels much better. Thank you, Lowry," she repeated. "Mercy, I need to stir the syrup! I don't want it to burn." She whisked to the stove.

Lowry looked after her with regret, and then he sighed. Years of dealing with little brothers and sisters had taught him that the moment was gone. He pointed, "Looky yonder on the table, Billy." Billy whooped and held the wooden boat aloft in triumphant hands. Lowry grinned. "Mandy, will you please excuse us while we go out to sail the boat for a while?"

In all the time Lowry had known her, he had never heard Amanda complain. She smiled and turned his heart to water. "Of course. The syrup needs to cool, so I'll come out, too, while the peaches drain. I'll put them in syrup later, let them lie all night, then dry them in the stove tomorrow."

That day sped by like many others as Lowry and Amanda strolled up and down the banks of the Ohio while Billy gripped the string of his boat.

Late one crisp November afternoon, Lowry smoothed a chestnut slab and watched long, pale curls of wood spiral to the floor. He picked one up and smiled; it reminded him of Amanda's golden ringlets. Lowry ran a finger over the chestnut; it was smooth as glass. Soon Uncle William would fit the carved end pieces to the pew bench Lowry was making for the new church. The intricate scrollwork gleamed with fresh varnish, but it was too late in the day to do more. Besides, he had strict instructions from Father to be home for supper, so he knew there must be a fugitive hidden somewhere. Father still expected Lowry to take his turn with his brothers in the "family business." He put on his wraps and said good-bye to Uncle William and Aunt Lucinda.

"Howdy, Mr. McCague!" he called cheerily as he passed the high front porch. It seemed like ages ago that he had hidden in that very lilac bush while Mr. James's slave escaped. Now the lilac was bare, the twigs covered with the buds of next spring's leaves. The sky was very clear and the air was still. Tonight promised to be clear and frosty.

"Evenin', Lowry." Mr. McCague's eyes twinkled. "Going over to the Kepharts? Got some chores to do?"

Lowry grinned. "No, sir. Goin' up to the Eminence for supper." That was what the people of Ripley called the Rankins' hill. Lowry had a feeling that Mr. McCague was the one with business for him later tonight, but he remembered Father's rule and did not ask.

When Lowry got home, however, he was surprised, because there was no fugitive to transport over the hill back of Ripley. All through dinner, there were no signal lights from town. For once, it looked like everyone was going to sleep well. Still, the Rankins always put a light in the upstairs window. Lowry lit the signal lamp at early candlelight and replaced the glass. He watched the flame flicker and then burn steadily. Who would see the signal tonight, he wondered? He sat on the edge of the bed for a long time and gazed at the constellations in the clear November sky. Orion's sword and scabbard glittered, the Pleiades huddled in a dim frightened shimmer, the Big Dipper poured stars across black velvet, and Polaris shone steadily in the north.

Chapter 7

A YOUNG MAN STOOD ON A hill above the Tuckahoe pike road in Kentucky and gazed across the wide river. His worth at eighteen was considerable, but not as a man. "If I stay here, I will always be a slave," he whispered. No one answered, for he spoke to the indifference of the spent foliage, the drab grays and browns of the dying autumn. He lifted his chin as he remembered that the One who had fashioned him heard his words. How did it go, that verse from Mr. Rankin's Bible school? "And ye shall know the truth, and the truth shall make you free." What did it mean? How should he go about it? He almost groaned aloud, he so yearned to be free.

Surely, freedom could not be that easy. Sometimes the verses that Mr. Rankin had taught confused him, but this one sounded so simple. He felt that God understood how he longed for freedom.

He gazed up at the Drinking Gourd. The bright stars on the right side of the gourd pointed to the North Star, constant in the sky, God's steadfast messenger to the unutterably weary. Across the Ohio, lamplight twinkled in a distant window as faithfully as the North Star in God's heaven. He meant to follow this light to freedom. All the slaves knew that John Rankin burned that light, and there was a stubborn rumor that he would help fugitives to freedom.

The young man came up here almost every night and wondered what it would be like to walk in that door. Would he see Lowry, his best friend from way back in Carlisle, Kentucky? What would happen next and how would he get free? If the rumors should prove to be just whispers in the wind, he knew he might be captured and sent down the river to hard labor in New Orleans, but that did not faze him. Something in that light beckoned to him, something almost holy, yet so intangible that he did not know what it could be. The idea shimmered and shifted, and then vanished.

He tried to reason it out. Ohio land lay the same as Kentucky land. Even the dividing river lapped carelessly at one shore and stretched to the other just as indifferently. The men, women, and children of one state looked like the people of the other. They even worshipped the same God in church on Sunday, and that thought often flummoxed him. There must be a difference, but for the life of him, he could not figure out what made one place a land of slavery and the other, only a half mile away, a land of freedom.

He shook his head and sighed. It was as if he peered through a bubbly glass window. Huff and polish as he might, the difference over there was hidden from him. He walked slowly down the hill, lost in thought. Who could tell him the truth about freedom? He made up his mind; he had to know, no matter what the cost.

Sherwood composed himself to face his master. He did not want to lie, but he had to be free. He must do it now, before his courage failed.

A quarter of an hour later, he held his breath and stood beside the fold-down writing surface of the narrow bookshelf secretary. Candlelight gleamed on the polished cherry wood. Sherwood remembered the day he had helped to carry it in the house. He could not guess how much Mr. Gilliam had paid for the desk, but he knew it was a high price, more money than Sherwood had ever seen. The piece had come special, all the way from Cincinnati. He glanced idly at the meaningless gilt letters on the spines of the fat books behind the glass and drew a deep breath. "Master Gilliam, sir, I needs a pass this evenin'."

Mr. Gilliam held up a finger as his plumed pen scratched and waved. Then he gave Sherwood his full attention. "Why, certainly Sherwood. Going to visit your gal like you been doin' every Satiddy night? Where does she live? It escapes me." Mr. Gilliam's face crinkled into a smile. "Beasley Creek, is that it? James's Marthy." He drew out the words.

Sherwood looked at his feet. "Yes, sir."

The master carefully blotted the pothooks and squiggles on the paper, and a roguish grin flickered. "Sherwood, don't be shy, now. You need to pop the question. Marthy's a fine gal, but she won't wait for you forever. Tell you what." Mr. Gilliam rubbed his whiskery chin. "I'll buy Marthy and keep her here. Will that hurry you along?"

Sherwood hoped Mr. Gilliam could not hear his knees knocking. Why did the man have to be so kind? It made it twenty times harder to run off, but Sherwood steeled himself. He had no idea why it was so hard to lie, when that lie was all that separated him from freedom. He glanced at the heavy silver porringer on the table. It held a helping of beef stew, the curls of steam misting the pierced tab that bore Mr. Gilliam's ornate monogram. The young man's stomach growled.

"Lordy, master." He swallowed hard and snickered. "You do go on! I'm jest a youngun. I cain't get hitched to no gal yet!"

The master threw up his hands. "Well, I've tried. Don't blame me if Marthy's spending time with a more likely prospect when you get there." Mr. Gilliam wrote out a pass that gave Sherwood the right to be out alone. If he did not have it, any patroller could pick him up and deal out ten lashes before he returned him to Mr. Gilliam for a reward. Mr. Gilliam had bought him from Mr. Roberts seven years ago, after the brutal beating by the stranger, back in Carlisle. He had not felt the cut of the whip since. Now he lived on Mr. Gilliam's prosperous plantation in Dover, on the Ohio River, and Sherwood had to admit that there was no kinder master in Kentucky. Few men would offer to buy Martha so Sherwood could legally marry her, though he knew most had the money.

Shame overwhelmed him. He opened his mouth to tell Mr. Gilliam the truth.

It was too late. The master handed him the precious pass. "Go on, Sherwood. I hope you will change your mind and marry Marthy. All it would take is one little question. Let me know. I'll see you Sunday evening." Just like that, the opportunity vanished, and he found himself alone on the doorstep in the November night.

His conscience pricked. He made up his mind; he would still run off, but he would not take the fine, soft suit that Mr. Gilliam had bought for him. How Marthy's eyes had shone when she saw him in that suit last Saturday! He walked to his cabin and hastily shucked off his boots and the garments before he could change his mind. Neatly he arranged them on the bed and shook out his rough tow field clothes, tattered though they were. He slipped them on and reached for his boots, but stopped. With a sigh, he lined them up by his bed. Well, he reasoned, he must live by his wits now. He certainly had no money to take along, and not even a crust of bread to his name.

He struck out in the direction of Beasley Creek. His bare feet squelched through the damp grass and were soon numb. The scratchy tow linen afforded little protection from the cold, and he rubbed his arms to ward off the chill. There was no moon, but by the faint starlight, he could see a skiff tied to a post. He sat down to wait for the slave hunters to be deep in their cups. It always happened so, later on Saturday nights. He tipped his hat over his eyes, laid his head on his knees, and drowsed.

Much later, water lapped at the skiff and he looked up at the stars. The Hunter strode high above as he chased the fleeing Seven Sisters across the sky. Sherwood thought of the slave hunters and a chill skittered down his back. He reassured himself that they were snoring unawares after a night of hard drinking. He knew by the stars that it must be well past two in the morning now. It was time to attend to his own work for today, the first free day of his life.

Sherwood crept forward and loosed the skiff. He was a few miles up the river from the Rankins' house. The lantern in the window glowed encouragingly as he paddled. With every stroke, he thought, "I'm going to be free."

The skiff bumped ashore at the mouth of Red Oak Creek, and he pushed it back out into the river. Maybe everyone would think he had drowned. He pushed down the notion that Mr. Gilliam would be devastated and stole through the blackjack oaks along the creek bed, toward the red brick house.

As he climbed the hill, a powerful thought exploded. "I'm free," he murmured in bewilderment. Joy coursed through him then and lent wings to his feet. He flew effortlessly up the steep rocky path, filled with joy unspeakable, for he must not cry out. He clapped his hand to his mouth.

It was no use. Joy bubbled up from deep within him and careened to the sky. It seemed he could *see* that joy now, golden and silver as it arced through the darkness. His mouth fell open. He dropped to his knees on the Rankins' doorstep and tipped his head back in awe. There strode the Hunter as always, and the Seven Sisters cowered in a frightened huddle. The Drinking Gourd dripped stars and the North Star winked, but the rest of the heavens split wide open as thousands of stars rained earthward.

The cascade of stars fizzed from a single point in the sky. They blazed so brightly that Sherwood cast a shadow. Stars zigzagged, and some even trailed smoke. Some crackled and hissed, and they fell thick and fast, like snowflakes in a blizzard. Goose bumps raised on his arms. Time stopped and he murmured, "My Lord and my God . . ."

He barely breathed the words, but someone standing in the doorway heard him and chimed, "Amen."

Sherwood jerked around in astonishment. A boy with a familiar pointy chin stood behind him. He blinked sleepily as he ran a hand through tousled yellow curls and yawned. "Y'all come on in," he invited.

"L-Lowry!" Sherwood stammered. "Don't you know me?"

The boy stared. "How do you—" he began, but he stopped. Sherwood saw recognition mingle with disbelief. "Sherwood? Is it you?" Seconds slipped by as the boy searched his face, and then Lowry grabbed his arm. "Come in quick. Y'all can't stay out here." Sherwood crossed the doorsill as the stars rained their fire and glory.

Lowry absentmindedly shoved kindling into the box stove until flames licked around the stove lids and the box glowed red. The boy kept sneaking peeks at him, as if he thought Sherwood was a ghost. A sudden chill rattled his teeth and made Lowry jump. He said, "Wait here. I'll get Father." He left Sherwood to warm himself and took the steps two at a time.

Sherwood looked around the simply furnished room. A spinning wheel stood in one corner, much polished with use. A desk made of tiger maple held a plain cut glass ink bottle and a goose-quill pen. A heavy book lay there, too, and there was a rocking chair in easy reach of the desk. The lines of the furniture were very different from what Mr. Gilliam had in his house, but somehow they seemed to welcome Sherwood in a manner he had never felt back home.

Soon he heard a commotion on the stairs, and then the rich, mellow voice from his Bible school days rang through the house. "David, Calvin, up like bucks! I have business for you! And wait until you look outside!"

Sherwood smiled. It amazed him that such a big sound came from such a small man. Boots clattered on the stairs, and then his old Bible school teacher was in the room. Dark hair waved back from his high forehead, and strong cheekbones accented his smooth-shaven face. His nose was long and straight. His mouth was a prim whip slash and he looked stern save for his warm blue eyes. The corners of his mouth turned up and then his eyes crinkled kindly while color flooded his handsome face.

"Oh, Sherwood!" There were tears in Mr. Rankin's eyes. Sherwood positively towered over the minister, who folded him in a bear hug of surprising strength. He looked way up at him. "I can scarcely believe it! How are you?"

"I'm all right. But I want to be free." His voice cracked as he finally said it aloud.

"Who can blame you?" Mr. Rankin murmured.

Sherwood removed his hat and his fingers worked nervously round his hat brim. He shook his head. "Mr. Rankin, back in Carlisle, Kentucky, I heard you and Mr. Roberts talk about slaves as few white folks talk, like we was people. I just want to know how to get to Canada. If you can't help me," he paused and screwed up his courage, "I've got a pass until Monday morning, and I'll get back home somehow." He paused again, and on the simple maple desk, he now recognized the big book as the familiar heavy Bible from which Mr. Rankin had taught the Bible school lessons so long ago. That Bible verse! Now he could find out what it meant, if he hurried. Mr. Rankin looked expectantly at him, but it was too late. Two boys clomped down the stairs, and the chance was gone.

"David, Calvin, my good friend Sherwood desires to go to Canada. Please saddle a horse for Lowry and Old Sorrel for this young man. He is an old friend of your brother's from Carlisle, so I expect they have some catching up to do." They shrugged on their wraps and stepped outside. Mr. Rankin grinned to hear their startled exclamations when they saw the sky. Then he called, "Ibby!"

Sherwood watched as his old teacher knocked on a door in the next room. A girl with a thin face and frail shoulders emerged and nudged the door shut as she swiftly braided her long brown hair. A certain set to her mouth made Sherwood think she might be stubborn. She looked him in the eye and smiled, though, and her whole face softened when Mr. Rankin spoke. "Sherwood needs a good meal, daughter. He has a long, chilly ride ahead." Pots rattled as Ibby took them from the warming oven.

A blaze of light brighter than fire lit the room. Mr. Rankin grew even more agitated, and two spots of red mottled his cheeks. "Wait a moment, Ibby. Hightail it outside! I have never seen anything like the spectacle in the heavens this morning, and I don't want you to miss it. You can tell your grandchildren about it someday."

Sherwood watched Ibby throw open the door. Her plain face lit up with delight. "Oh, Father!" she gasped. "It's lovely! What is it?"

"A shower of meteors. I have never seen one greater. We will long remember this night in 1833. Well, well, Sherwood, none of this will get you to Canada. Give him something to eat when you have looked your fill, daughter." He climbed the stairs.

"I don't think I would ever grow tired of watching this," she sighed. She walked back to the stove. "Mercy me, who put in so much wood?" She busied herself with the damper.

Sherwood stole a glance at Lowry. His friend silently motioned to the long table in the other room, and after he handed Sherwood a tin cup full of water, they both sat down. Ibby brought a wooden trencher of mush and milk and left the room. Sherwood wolfed the food down unashamedly. Still Lowry did not speak, and Sherwood smiled uncertainly. "How you been, Lowry?"

For a long second, their gazes held, then Lowry looked away. There was an awkward difference in him. His face turned red, and Sherwood cocked his head and grinned. "What's the matter? Don't feel bad just 'cause I let you beat me that day we raced to the schoolhouse. I reckon you ran your best, son." He drew the last word out in his best Kentucky taunt.

Lowry's eyebrows drew together. "You never let me win! I beat you fair and square!" he shot back.

"Do tell!" Sherwood laughed and punched him on the arm. A foolish grin spread over Lowry's face. At last, he looked like the good friend Sherwood remembered. "You just the same, always ready to butt heads like a billy goat." He picked up the tin cup and drained it, then wiped his mouth on his sleeve. "You forget how to laugh, Lowry?"

"Maybe I just don't have much to laugh about." The minute the words came out, Lowry hung his head. Sherwood could tell he was ashamed at the difference in their lives.

"Don't worry your head about me, Lowry." He searched for the words to tell his friend that he understood. "Mr. Gilliam's been a good master. I lived mighty fine there." Sherwood thought again of the rich trappings in the Gilliam house. There was no silver porringer at the Rankins' table, just a wooden trencher worn smooth with repeated use. "He even offered to buy my gal, so's we could get married. I sure wish I could have done it. I love that gal." Sherwood sighed ruefully. "It was only that one time in my life, back in Carlisle, that another man got me under his thumb, and that was the only cowhidin' I ever got. I been lucky.

"But you know what, Lowry?" Sherwood's attention wandered and he traced a white-ridged scar on his arm. "I found out that Mr. Roberts didn't own me, after all. I belonged to *Mrs.* Roberts. Mr. Roberts never would have done it otherwise, but he sold me on 'count of his brother-in-law owed money. It wasn't because of the cowhidin'."

"I'm s-sorry." Lowry's eyes glistened and his mouth worked as if he wanted to say more, but no words came.

"It ain't your doin'."

Lowry shook his head. "You don't know . . ." he stopped and glanced over his shoulder, but Ibby was out of earshot. "I'm a coward. I tried to forget about what happened to you. I know I should speak up about it, some way," Lowry gulped. "Slavery, I mean, but I can't."

"Shoot, son, you ain't no coward. I'll never forget hearin' how you saved Ibby from that hog." Lowry waved his hand feebly to dismiss that, but Sherwood went on, "I try to forget about that cowhidin', too, ever' day, but I can't, neither." He sighed. "That's why I run off. There ain't no kinder master than Mr. Gilliam is, and it was mighty hard to lie to him, but no tellin' when it might happen again. Cowhidin' or worse, I mean, from some stranger who don't even know me, but just hate me because of what I look like."

"Or what I sound like," Lowry muttered, but his voice was so low that Sherwood was not sure he heard right.

"Or for what we believe." Sherwood jumped about as high as Lowry did. How long had Mr. Rankin been in the room? He did not say anything else. He put a hand on each boy's head. "Everything's ready. It's time, Lowry."

"Mr. Rankin, I can't ride a horse very well," Sherwood hedged. He heard the jingle of bridles and the *whoosh* of the horses as they blew and stamped.

Mr. Rankin waved aside his protests. "My friend, riding Old Sorrel is the easiest thing you will do tonight. He knows just what he is about, and he loves his work. As for the rest of the trip, you will be escorted all the way to Canada now, for there are friends at every station on the way. All you have to do is follow," Mr. Rankin reassured. The minister's face flamed with excitement. He mopped his brow.

Ibby came back with dark fabric draped over her arm. She opened a crock and handed Sherwood some doughnuts. "Put them in your pocket for later," she urged. Then she held up an old surtout with neatly patched elbows.

"I believe this will fit you, and it is cold tonight," she said. "What do you think, Lowry?" But Lowry only nodded, as if he did not trust himself to speak.

"Thank you." Sherwood's voice was low.

"You are very welcome, and God go with you, friend," she smiled.

Sherwood watched her leave the room. Tears sprang to his eyes and he passed a shaky hand across his face as he thought about leaving. Lowry looked miserable, too, and uneasy, like he could not make up his mind about something.

Sherwood noticed the Bible again. The sight triggered the tantalizing image of the bubbly glass that warped his vision and prevented him from seeing the difference, the difference that made him a slave *there,* but a free man *here*. Puzzled, he shook his head. Now, why had he thought of that again?

Lowry gritted his teeth, brushed past Sherwood, and opened the Bible. The gilded edges caught the fire's golden light. Lowry's hand shook as he moved it down the page. He cleared his throat, and then he stood tall.

"And ye shall know the truth, and the truth shall make you free," he read. He looked up. "Once you asked me what that meant. I couldn't say then, but I can now. Do you know the truth yet, Sherwood?" Lowry's eyes were steady if his hands were not.

Sherwood drew in his breath sharply. He felt like he was choking. Lowry remembered! He shook his head. "I don't know," he rasped.

Lowry carefully turned a few more pages. He read, "'Jesus saith unto him, I am the way, the truth, and the life: no man cometh unto the Father, but by me.' He is the truth, Sherwood. Jesus is the difference," he said simply. His eyes shone as if the weight of the world was off his shoulders.

Warmth tingled to the tips of Sherwood's toes. Mr. Rankin placed a hand on each of his shoulders and looked into his eyes. "It is a narrow way, Sherwood," he said, and his voice held an unmistakable warning. "There will be many sacrifices. Just look to Jesus."

Sherwood saw Lowry cock his head at Mr. Rankin, like there was something he did not understand. No matter—Sherwood wanted to leap and sing and shout! He meant to get better acquainted with Jesus, now that he was free.

"Well, Lowry, come along." Mr. Rankin held the back door open. "You boys can talk more on the way. Good-bye, Sherwood. God go with you." Mr. Rankin paused. He hugged Lowry hard, and when he let him go, Sherwood saw tears in the minister's eyes, or maybe his own tears blurred his sight. One thing he knew for sure—he would never forget the night that his friend had told him about the Truth.

Chapter 8

Lowry rested his chin on his hands and stared at the drawing before him. Why should it be so difficult to finish this plan for a staircase? He raised his arms above his head, stretched, and felt a muscle twinge from the carpentry work on the *Fair Play* that morning. He rubbed his stomach. Dinner smelled wonderful—he must remember to tell Aunt Lucinda. He stood up, walked to the window, and stared out at nothing.

There was no use denying it. Since his reunion with Sherwood, Lowry felt different about his drafting apprenticeship. No matter what happened, the vague uneasiness grew more defined. Even the May emergence of a horde of seventeen-year locusts failed to rouse him, though their deafening, eerie call of "Pha-a-a-raoh" blotted out every other sound. Lowry thanked God that the locusts did not sing after nightfall. After a month, the dying cicadas laid the eggs for the new brood, which would not emerge until 1851. Lowry's new little sister Lucinda, named for her aunt, would be seventeen years old by then, but she was red, wrinkled, and hungry right now, as he had discovered on a weekend visit home.

He read new books that he borrowed from a friend in town. His favorites of 1834 were very different. One was *The Narrative of the Life of David Crockett*, the congressman's autobiography. The book made interesting reading, especially since Lowry was from the same area of Tennessee as Crockett. He was a person Lowry admired because of Crockett's brave stand against the Indian Removal Act of 1830, President Jackson's shameful attempt to seize the gold fields discovered in Dahlonega, Georgia. The Indians had appealed the order, but suppose the Cherokees and other tribes still had to leave their ancestral lands, all over the discovery of gold? Lowry shook his head in disgust. Whatever the outcome, he liked Crockett's adage, "Be always sure you are right, then go ahead."

Another book he read late that year was *The Last Days of Pompeii*, by Edward George Bulwer-Lytton. Lowry lived the story with the characters, right up until Mt. Vesuvius erupted and buried the entire city alive.

Meanwhile, Lowry faced his own smothering Vesuvius—he was consumed with the desire to know whether Sherwood was safe, but there was no one to ask. He must trust the Lord, but the strain told on him. Most days it was a struggle just to get out of bed as his troubles simmered beneath his determined cheerfulness. His craftsmanship suffered, too; he had seen Uncle William look askance at his work more than once.

Lately Lowry's frustration had grown, and he thought he could put a finger on the trouble. Theodore Weld's revival at Father's church had given Ripley a new heart for abolition, something Lowry had never thought would happen to the sharply divided town. But Ripley had not reckoned on Mr. Weld and his powerful message. Lowry guessed that Mr. Weld could even talk water into flowing uphill, if he took the notion.

They had never heard a speaker like him, he and Amanda agreed. The way he spoke with such love about the free black people of Cincinnati made Lowry wish he knew them, too. He could understand why nearly the entire student body of Lane Seminary, Dr. Lyman Beecher's school in Cincinnati, had rallied around Weld after the Lane Slavery Debates.

For eighteen nights last February, while Dr. Beecher gathered funds back east, the students debated the slavery issue, and, as moderator, Weld patiently heard both sides. By the end, he convinced many who opposed abolition to change their minds, and he even swayed those who favored colonization, the halfway solution that meant sending freed slaves to Liberia, over abolition, which meant freeing two million slaves to roam America. The verdict was in; the students favored abolition.

The resulting uproar threw Cincinnati, the last civilized town at the western edge of the United States, into a frenzy. The *Western Messenger* newspaper printed editorials couched with incendiary rhetoric in support of slavery, which Weld refuted gently and logically in the *Cincinnati Journal*. A few letters supported Weld, and Father himself had written one of the longest and most eloquent of these. He urged Dr. Beecher to support the students, but Dr. Beecher was in a difficult position, and he chose peace rather than reform. For their part, the Lane students formed an abolition society and mingled freely with the black community, eager to show brotherly love in any way possible.

The students had not reckoned with the seminary trustees, however. The trustees demanded no further discussion on the slavery matter, disbanded the new abolition society, and ordered the students to cease their humanitarian efforts among the three thousand black residents of Cincinnati. The students were to comply or be dismissed.

On a day Father still talked about with reverence, Theodore Weld and all the students but five resigned, gathered their belongings, and walked out of Lane Seminary forever. Now they attended Oberlin College in northern Ohio, a new school that supported the anti-slavery cause. More importantly, Oberlin College accepted black students as well as white, and boasted the abolitionist minister Charles Finney as its president.

Recently matters had settled enough that Father had invited Mr. Weld to hold a revival in Ripley. As a result, Lowry and many others belonged to the new Ripley and Red Oak Anti-Slavery Society. So many had signed the charter that the slaveholders over in Kentucky had a special name for Ripley now; they called the village "that rat's nest of abolition."

Did signing a charter solve the problem? A few citizens, Lowry included, were not satisfied. Their eyes were opened to the anti-slavery cause as never before. Deep down, Lowry knew that Mr. Weld was right. Slavery must be abolished. The catch was how to achieve it. How could one person *do* something about so huge an issue? A wave of helplessness overwhelmed Lowry. He left the window and descended to the shop.

The talk in the shop that December day had been all about the arrival of the new steamer, the *Uncle Sam*, due in from Pittsburgh on its way to New Orleans. Everyone wanted to see it. Uncle William cheerfully granted permission for work to cease as soon as the steamer docked.

At last, Lowry heard a blast from a whistle and dashed out of the shop. The big new steamer nosed her way cautiously downriver as scores of Ripley residents teemed along the wharf in eager anticipation. Someone jostled him and apologized, "Sorry, Lowry! Going aboard?"

He recognized a new friend and laughed, "Try and stop me!" Together they walked up the gangplank. Now that the pressure of school was off, Lowry felt a bit more at ease socially and even chatted with people as he wandered around the work deck of the *Uncle Sam*. Old habits died hard, though, and he split off from the others in his group when he passed the staircase to the upper passenger deck. He rubbed his hands together; now maybe he could see where he had gone wrong with his own design. He studied the way the staircase fit into the space as he ascended, but for the life of him, he could not put his finger on the problem. The staircase to the topmost "Texas" deck, where the gentry traveled, only perplexed him more. Lost in thought, he took the stairs back down and found himself near the engine room on the work deck. There he heard a sound like crying and caught his breath.

He saw a narrow room on a bare wooden deck. Usually the room between the engine room and the boiler might be filled with horses, or other large cargo that would not fit in the shallow hold beneath the main deck. There were no horses here now. A long, heavy chain ran the length of the outside walls, bolted to them about four feet above the floor. Every four inches he saw shorter lengths of chain like the ones he used to hitch Old Sorrel to the plow. At the end of each of these chains was an iron cuff, and each cuff was clamped around the wrist of a slave. Nauseated, he counted twenty-five battered men on one side of the room and twenty-five women on the other, one pitifully crippled. Some of them hunkered down; some lay stretched upon the deck, and some stood. Lowry saw many clenched fists on the men's side of the room.

As he sidled along the wall to escape, he glimpsed a white girl about Amanda's age chained with the others. He stopped and gaped in consternation. The folds of her fashionable dress shimmered and hid her chained right hand. Her glossy black hair was dressed in ringlets that highlighted the shining silkiness. She covered her face with a soft white hand, and her slim shoulders heaved as she cried. Her head came up as she caught a shaky breath, and Lowry saw that she was very beautiful.

The very air pressed against him until he could not breathe. "Can it be?" he whispered. "Can it be that she is a slave?" He studied her tear-stained face. She was as white as he was. Well, he reasoned to himself, she looks white, but she must be part African, because you can't sell a white girl as a slave. He felt better for a moment, but then he was ashamed. What difference did it make? White, black, or in-between, should this girl—or anyone—be a slave? He wrestled with the thought, uncertain how to handle this new revelation. He half-turned to go.

"Ain't she a beauty?" Lowry stepped back further. He saw two men now standing almost abreast of him and staring at the same girl.

The slovenly older one must be a slave trader, Lowry judged, because plantation owners in general were a better class of people than this man. He smelled of whiskey, too, and his long, greasy hair stuck to his neck. His broad-brimmed hat was pulled down to hide all but his cruel mouth. He wore heavy woolen clothes, with the tops of his trousers tucked into thick-soled cowhide boots caked with mud. Lowry knew that slaves lived in fear of traders, and most plantation holders viewed them as a necessary evil at best. Certainly, the man did not attempt to endear himself to the object of his sales pitch. Lowry leaned forward for a better look at the other man.

He was very tall and well dressed, and he carried himself gracefully. Lowry noted his chiseled jaw, cleanly shaven, and the carefully brushed wavy hair. The young man's clothing gleamed down to his spotless leather shoes. His language and manners bespoke fine training at home, for he used no profanity. For all his height, a certain boyishness lingered about his sensitive mouth. He looked like a guilty child caught with his finger in the sugar bowl. He seemed a very young Southern gentleman to Lowry. In fact, he typified Lowry's memory of most of the slaveholders he had known in Kentucky: God-fearing family men of good repute in all respects, except somehow their better judgment was clouded concerning slavery. He marveled that an individual of such obvious good breeding and taste should associate with the likes of this slave trader.

"Well, what do you think of this little gal, son?" The slave trader licked his thick lips. As they strolled toward the frightened girl, he continued, "Ain't she all that ever I said she was? I could get three thousand for her easily in New Orleans. Matter of fact, I know other . . ." he looked the young man up and down and sneered, "*men* who would jump at the chance I'm offering you for only twenty-five hundreds of dollars. It ain't too much for a gal as looks like her, now, is it?" he asked, as they stopped before the girl. She trembled.

An angry sibilance of curses broke out, and several of the black men stepped forward as far as their chains allowed at the slave trader's words. The other women sobbed and pleaded. The girl shuddered. Her beautiful face froze into a dreadful mask.

Lowry could see that the young man was sorely tempted. Sweat popped out on his forehead, but he swallowed hard and shook his head. "I only have two thousand, sir," he whispered hoarsely, yet he did not turn to go. He was so shaken that he could not take his eyes from the girl. He reached as if to brush away her tears, then he dropped his hand to his side.

Thank you, Lord, Lowry thought. A chorus of whispered amens broke out down the line of slaves.

"That's enough, you black whelps!" roared the slave trader. He swung the rawhide cane high and slashed the girl's shoulder. "Hush that noise or I will half-kill you!" he raged. The young man flinched. The slave trader saw his mistake and quickly changed his tactics. He dug a dirty finger under the girl's chin and applied pressure until she looked him in the eye.

He whispered something in her ear, and the chain rattled as the terrified girl raised her hands in a silent plea. The cane whistled through the air again and struck her other shoulder. "Do it!"

"Please, no," she begged, and Lowry could not bear her gentle anguish. The slave trader struck her with the cane once more and she did as she was bidden.

Walk away, Lowry thought. *Now is the time to walk away, before it's too late.* He willed the young man to comply, but nothing happened. Dimly he knew that he must act, that he should rush in with a splendid show of courage and *do* something, just as he had when the boar attacked Ibby, when Mr. James's slave escaped—but he could not think what to do. In the next instant, the slave trader snatched at the girl with cruel hands and Lowry turned away. Moments later, the jingle of gold coins and the dull clank as the cuff of the chain thudded to the floor told him all he needed to know. Shame flooded over Lowry.

Sick with revulsion, he dashed to the gangplank and elbowed his way to shore. In the twilight, Ripley tended to business as usual, unaware of the wickedness in the hold of the *Uncle Sam*. Lowry breathed hard and raised his right hand toward heaven. Right there, he made a promise aloud to God, for once not shy at all.

"My God helping me, there shall be a perpetual war between me and human slavery in this nation of which I am a member. I pray God I may never be persuaded to give up the fight until slavery is dead or the Lord calls me home." Angry tears spilled down his cheeks.

"Lowry, what is the matter? Do I hear you swearing?" a young friend asked in astonishment.

"Yes, what of it? I have made a solemn promise before God that I will fight slavery until it is dead."

His friend edged away. Plainly, he thought Lowry had lost his mind. He babbled, "Oh, well, that is all right, I suppose, but you will die long before slavery is killed!" He scuttled into the evening shadows.

Lowry grimaced and stalked to Uncle William's house. "What is the matter with me?" he muttered. His hands shook. "That young lady—I should have taken her away and out of the *Uncle Sam*, but I turned tail and ran like a coward."

He shoved open the door and it crashed against the wall. Uncle William and Aunt Lucinda appeared with frightened faces, but Lowry only snarled, "Excuse me, Aunt. I am not feeling well." He stormed up the stairs.

He saw his drawing board, where the unfinished sketch of the staircase mocked him. "You will never be a draftsman," he chided himself. He tore the sheet from top to bottom and flung it to the floor. "What of it, Lowry? Did you mean what you said to God out there? How will you keep your vow?" He held his head in his hands as one thought chased another. "Why didn't I help her?" he moaned. "I wanted to help, but I didn't! Slavery must die, yes, but do I believe that enough to act? If I can't speak to one person, how can I speak before a hundred? How can I be a minister?"

A powerful image of the beautiful girl in chains, beaten and shamed before his very eyes, haunted him. He knew that he could never forget her, or what she stood for. He bowed his head contritely.

His room was dark before he looked up again. "Well, I'm in for it now," he murmured ruefully. "How they will all laugh at me when I tell them I want to go to school to be an abolition minister, just what they said I should be! Everyone in town knew it before I did." He chuckled, and his heart lifted. Finally, he knew exactly what he was going to do with his life, and most important of all, he knew it was what God wanted, too.

Chapter 9

Lowry Rankin's reenrollment at Ripley College was the talk of the town. Bleakly, he attacked his books so he could make up what he had missed during his apprenticeship. By the time school let out, he had caught up with his class, but he still had another year to go, according to Father. No matter how Lowry pleaded, Father refused to allow Lowry to enter Lane Seminary before the fall of 1836.

Lowry had to admit that it was a pleasure to be back home on the farm, even though the work was as demanding as ever. Old Sorrel greeted him with a ringing whinny and eagerly threw his weight into the traces. A rich, familiar smell rose out of the damp earth as the soil curled aside in unbroken waves before the plowshare and the sun beat down on man and horse.

The other good news was that Amanda Kephart now lived at the Hayden Thompson place, the farm that adjoined the Rankins' land. Her eldest sister, Mary, had married Mr. Thompson, and Amanda's mother had brought the family up to live with them. Lowry saw Amanda often that summer because he helped Mr. Thompson mend fences.

In the evenings, lively debates raged at the supper table as the Rankins discussed the news of the day. The strangest story concerned a dispute between the state of Ohio and the Michigan territory over 486 acres of land along their common border called the Toledo Strip. Ohio's survey put the state line further north, but Michigan's survey set the line further south. Neither side would budge, and the papers had dubbed the conflict the Toledo War.

The Michigan territorial governor, Stevens T. Mason, was a youth of twenty-three, not much older than Lowry. When Mason brashly sent militia forces to defend the strip, Ohio governor Robert Lucas retaliated by sending his own forces into the area. President Andrew Jackson sent two commissioners to mediate the dispute, and the United States Congress eventually stepped in and awarded Toledo to Ohio. The victorious Ohioans named the newly formed Lucas County for Governor Lucas. As for the Michigan territory, they were awarded the relatively worthless western two-thirds of the Upper Peninsula for their trouble.

By the Fourth of July, there was a noteworthy item about the Baltimore and Ohio Railroad. Workers had completed the Thomas Viaduct at Relay, Maryland. The bridge was the longest in the United States and the second longest in the world; only London Bridge was longer. In seven years, however, only seven miles of the B & O Railroad had been completed. Lowry did not hold out much hope for the future of the railroad industry.

There was little in the news about the Cincinnati abolitionists in 1835. Lowry hoped the chaos might subside once the Lane agitators were gone, but in 1836, the mood soon turned ugly. Trouble flared up when publisher James Birney teamed with printer Achilles Pugh to publish *The Philanthropist*, which came to be seen by Cincinnatians as the radical voice of the Ohio Anti-Slavery Society. Not long after the newspaper's debut on January 1, 1836, business leaders in Newport and Covington, over on the Kentucky side of the river, as well as several in Cincinnati itself, plotted to suppress *The Philanthropist.* By January 22, Cincinnati mayor Samuel Davies held an organizational meeting for that purpose at the Hamilton County Courthouse.

Lowry had to admire James Birney—the man had not only shown up for the meeting called to banish him, but asked if he could speak, too. At first, his request outraged the dockworkers and Kentucky toughs gathered outside. "Kill him! Kill him!" they screamed, but Birney spoke so persuasively that the meeting broke up without incident.

Words alone could not stop the violence against black citizens, however, and rioters persisted in their efforts to drive out those whom they saw as the root of the problem. Lowry knew that Father believed that Cincinnati's argument against abolition was based more on pocketbooks than morals. He said that Cincinnati merchants valued their business relationship with Kentucky and the South above their compunctions about slavery. They supposed the whole town would shut down if slavery were abolished.

On July 30, tensions exploded. A mob gathered outside Pugh's print shop, where they resolved to stop publication of *The Philanthropist* and run Birney and Pugh out of town. The two men were nowhere to be found, so the angry mob stormed the print shop, tossing bales of newsprint and dumping trays of type out the windows. "Burn it all!" someone gleefully suggested, but cooler heads prevailed. A bonfire might endanger other desirable businesses nearby, they said. When they could not find Birney or Pugh, and they were prevented from starting a bonfire, the frustrated rioters came up with a new plan—they smashed the printing press itself, dragging a portion of it down Main Street and pitching it into the Ohio River. Amid the mayhem, they watched warily for Mayor Davies or the constable to arrive, but no one appeared to stop the violence.

Next, the mob raced to James Birney's house, but they were frustrated again when he was not at home. "What's to stop us from cleaning out Church Alley?" the cry arose, and the rioters moved en masse to the nearby neighborhood of black citizens. Here they destroyed the homes of two prominent black families before their anger subsided.

What amazed Lowry as he read the news accounts of the riot

was that some of Cincinnati's most respected citizens had participated side-by-side with the city's riffraff. With a sigh, he folded the newspaper and blew out the lamp. It seemed that not a day passed without violence breaking out somewhere.

October 1836 soon rolled around and Lowry's life entered a new phase. Tomorrow he would leave home to begin his new endeavor. Everything he would need at Lane Seminary was packed and ready to go.

The family held a midweek prayer service to pray for Lowry. Then, one by one, his brothers climbed the stairs to go to bed and his sisters retired to their room downstairs. Mother stayed up a long time with Tappan, the latest Rankin baby. She joggled him back and forth as she reminisced with Lowry. Father shook his hand and was uncharacteristically silent. Lowry felt there was nothing left to say—besides, Father would travel with him to Cincinnati.

On his way to bed, Lowry passed the girls' room, where Ibby and Julia shared one bed, and Mary and their adopted cousin, Almira, shared the other. He climbed the stairs. On the right was Mother and Father's room. He could not hear Lucinda or William; they must already be asleep in the trundle bed. Tappan still fussed, though, and Lowry heard Mother's low murmur as she soothed the youngest Rankin while she rocked his cradle.

Lowry pulled open the door to his room. He had to walk carefully in the dark, because two big beds practically filled the room. Samuel, Johnny, and Andrew slept in the newer bed, which Lowry had built. He dressed quickly and eased into his bed, next to David in the middle, with Calvin against the wall.

Lowry clasped his hands behind his head and listened to the gentle snores of his brothers. Soon he would have a bed to himself.

He grinned. For once, he had turned the tables and teased David mercilessly at supper. "Don't you wish you could go to Cincinnati, where a man can stretch out when he sleeps?" He knew Samuel would take the space Lowry vacated, and then William could move out of the trundle bed he shared with Lucinda to sleep with Johnny and Andrew. David had the last laugh, though, when he reminded Lowry that it was his turn to build up the stove in the morning, since Lowry would sleep to the outside of the bed one last time.

Of course, this was not the first time Lowry had left home. He had slept in a bed of his own at Uncle William's house. This time, however, he would be fifty miles away from Ripley and his family. He would miss them, he knew, but what bothered him most was that he would also be fifty miles away from Amanda. He and Amanda had said their good-byes yesterday, and she had promised to write.

After Lowry waved farewell to what looked like everyone in Ripley, the voyage downriver to Cincinnati passed in a whirl. Before he knew it, the *Fair Play* chuffed around a hill at the bend of the Ohio River and revealed the city that was the gateway to the uncivilized west. "There it is, son. Cincinnati will be your home for the next few months. What do you think of her?" Father asked.

Lowry gripped the rail and leaned forward for a better look. He saw a wide, paved public landing that sloped gently up from the river. More steamships than he had ever seen at once rocked on the current. White clouds sailed overhead across a powder blue October sky, and wisps of smoke rose from thousands of chimneys. Up ahead, the river curved northward around the west edge of the town, which was nestled among several blue hills visible in the distance. Cincinnati was beautiful!

"There are so many buildings," he said in wonder. Father answered, but a blast of the steam whistle drowned out his words and Lowry laughed. Father grinned and clapped his shoulder.

"I said, 'Let's go to our cabin and get our things,'" he repeated. They made their way along the deck while everywhere muscular stevedores bustled to unload uncured cowhides and slabs of pork and load up empty sugar hogsheads to send down to New Orleans. It seemed that the *Fair Play*, which Lowry had helped build at Ripley, was hardly large enough to hold it all, though Lowry knew the deck was one hundred feet long and twenty feet wide. He watched the two magnificent sidewheels churn the water.

"I wonder how much steam she carries?" he asked Father.

The steward overheard him. "I can answer that, sir," he replied. "The *Fair Play* has two thirty-five horsepower steam engines." Pride showed in his sunburned face.

Always interested in the workings of machinery, Lowry was eager to show his knowledge. "How many woodcutters does it take to keep her running?"

"There are thirteen, sir, and four stokers to chuck it into the boilers."

"That must be hot work on such a warm day," Father put in. "Those men have a hard job."

The steward shrugged and the corners of his mouth turned down. "I'm sure they work no harder than the rest of us. We have a crew of thirty-one, all told."

"How much wood does it take to keep the engines going for one day?" Lowry persisted. He knew it took a lot, for he had sold wood to the steamships in Ripley since the time he was small. Steam engines were insatiable.

"Well," the man sniffed disdainfully, "I've heard that it takes about forty cords for thirty miles, which is what we make in a day. Of course, I have nothing to do with that side of the business."

"Forty cords!" Lowry whistled. He thought of all the work it took to cut one cord of firewood, a stack four feet high, four feet wide, and eight feet long. "So that means it has taken us the better part of eighty cords to come the fifty miles from Ripley."

The steward sounded curt. "Yes, but why go on about it? Now if you will excuse me, I have important business to attend to."

Before Lowry could say anything else, the man was gone. Behind Father, a stevedore knotted together a bundle of green hides and sidled to stand beside him. "Pay no mind to Mr. Babcock." His blue eyes sparkled in his suntanned face. "Go see the boiler for yourself! It's like the jaws of Hades. It's a wonder those poor black brutes have any hair left, and they can't get the smell of fire offen them at night. Stoking's not a job I would take, not for any amount of money." He shook his head and got back to work. Lowry stared after him thoughtfully.

"Come, Lowry." Father looked at him sidewise. "Don't let that steward get your goat. He was just pulling rank. Haven't you noticed that the deck crew and the stevedores are white, but the cabin crews and firemen are colored?"

Lowry shook his head. He had to admit that Father was right, as always. Even on a steamship called the *Fair Play*, the color of your skin made a difference.

They joined the crowd waiting to go ashore. When they disembarked, Lowry loaded his trunk on the luggage rack of a bright red stagecoach with an undercarriage painted yellow to hide road dust. The driver, a friendly fellow with lank black hair, a hooked nose, and a lazy eye, motioned to Lowry and patted the seat to his left. Lowry clambered to perch beside the man. Father, preferring to ride inside the coach, mounted the folding steps and entered the cabin.

"This your first trip to the Queen of the West?" the driver asked as Lowry settled into his seat. Lowry nodded. Cincinnati's nickname had been around for twenty years, long enough for Ripley folk to know it. "Generally, my messenger sits here next to me," the driver continued. "He's paid to guard the cash box and shoot to kill, and I'm paid to drive. That's when we travel overland, though. I don't use a messenger in town."

The driver chirruped to his six horses and the stagecoach jolted. The six horses clopped steadily through the heavy wet clay streets. Lowry wished he could cover his nose to filter out the smells that rose from the street; he had never smelled anything like it, even on Ripley's worst day. He did not want to appear rude, so he suffered in silence. He wondered if Father, somewhat sheltered inside the carriage, was laughing at him right now.

A huge drift of hogs swarmed the street. Lowry watched the unruly procession of slab-sided animals with mild interest until his attention was captured by two drovers who struggled with one squirming, wayward, dirty white hog. A dog yipped and nipped at the hog's hocks as the men wrestled the animal to its side. "This'll larn ye to run away!" Lowry heard, and then a horrible squeal. One man knelt on the hog's side and squeezed its eyelids together while the other man sewed them shut. It was done like lightning; the hog was up and blundering about in an instant. It dared not leave the drift now because it could not see, and the drovers were on their merry way with hoarse shouts to the dogs. Lowry felt sick.

The driver drew a deep, unconcerned breath and sighed. "Ah, Cincinnati!" He pointed at the hill to the east of the landing. "That there's Mount Ida." A happy grin covered his ugly but good-natured face. Lowry decided to make the best of the situation. He admired aloud the way the driver handled the reins.

"Well, now, I call 'em ribbons, but I thank you. There's not many as appreciates a good driver." His eyes scanned the road ahead; he never looked directly at Lowry. "Name's Charlie Bryson. All stagecoach drivers are called Charlie, but I like that name better'n my own." His hands barely moved as he subtly telegraphed his wishes to the lead horses. He held the near horses' lines in his left hand, each between separate fingers, with the slack trailing. The off horses' lines he held in his right hand, with the whip perfectly balanced between his thumb and index finger. A twinkle of light caught Lowry's eye. The handle was inlaid with silver.

Lowry wondered how the man could manage the whip. As if in answer, Bryson winked, "Any horse I need to use a whip on ain't fit to be in my team. We only use the best horses. The heavy ones in front—they're called the leaders. They're smart. Middle 'uns are the swings, and these nighest are the wheelers."

The driver nodded at a line of buildings. "Yonder's Cassilly's Row. Mr. Cassilly owns all them buildings, and he has his own dry goods store here on Front Street." *Another Front Street, right along the river, just like at home*, Lowry thought. The driver skimmed the brake with his right foot and his right index finger twitched. The leaders snapped back their ears and swung right in a wide arc to travel north up the broad avenue, and the others followed without a hitch. "This here's Broadway Street. See them two big buildings?"

"Those two, a block apart?"

"Them's the ones. Now, that there's Cromwell's, what he calls the Cincinnati Hotel, and that one's called the Broadway Hotel. Reckon you heard about our big flood four years ago, back in '32, that was. Well, between Cassilly's Dry Goods, the Cincinnati, and the Broadway—the hotels had twenty inches of water in their barrooms downstairs, and water covered the floors in the western stores of Cassilly's buildings. Water filled the space between the two hotels. The Ohio was swelled to a mile from shore to shore and seventy feet deep. That's the honest truth, or my name ain't Bryson!" The man cocked his head and waited for his reaction, so Lowry gave a low, appreciative whistle.

The driver grinned. Lowry wondered how long it had been since the man had found someone to listen to him. He talked to Lowry as if he were a long-lost friend. For that matter, Lowry felt the same way. This man and Father were the only souls he knew in Cincinnati.

Bryson adjusted the lines. "Reason I know," he went on, "is I drive a lawyer fellow around quite regular, and he told me so. Name's Salmon P. Chase. Why, he told me that he hired a waterman to *row* him down Elm Street to Front Street. Said he had the waterman stop the boat so's he could talk with some young ladies he knew lived down on Front Street between Elm and Plum. They was hangin' out the second-story window, if you can b'lieve it, gabbin' a blue streak, and him in the boat easy as you please, but he said their front door was open and their parlor was under water."

"That's amazing!" Lowry looked at the driver with new respect. He certainly knew a lot about Cincinnati.

The next instant, the driver hauled the ribbons violently to the right, set the brake, and jumped to the ground. In a flash, he was at the near leader's side. He held the cheek-strap and murmured in the horse's ear as the nervous animal pranced. Then Lowry heard a great commotion as a runaway horse with ears pinned back plunged into view around the corner, the dray it hauled careening behind it. The poor horse was lathered with sweat and wall-eyed with fear. Heavy wooden barrels of apples slewed off the open sides of the dray and burst open in the street like firecrackers. The apples rolled everywhere, and pandemonium broke out as the hogs squealed and slobbered over them with greedy delight. The unruffled stagecoach driver rejoined Lowry to pick his way through the wreckage.

Bryson's weathered eyes creased into a smile. "Shucks, I love it here in the Queen of the West. D'ya see all them steamers in the harbor back where you got off? Now warn't that a beautiful sight? Most days, there's fifty or more, loading up. They put off tobacco, sugar, cotton, ammunition, fancy clothes, most all from down New Orleans way. We mostly ship out grain and livestock. Doin' a boomin' business in furniture and silver goods, too, though." He paused. "See here, I been doing all the talkin'. What about you? What do you want to know?" He asked with the confidence of a man who would know the answer.

"Well," Lowry suddenly felt shy. "I've come to go to school. I want to be a minister."

"Now, that's fine. Where you going to school?"

"Lane Seminary."

The stagecoach driver's lazy eye bobbed disconcertingly. "Lane Seminary? What you want to go there for?" he asked. The stagecoach hit a rut and took a nasty jounce.

"To be a—" he began, but Bryson interrupted him.

"You one a' them abolitionists?"

Every muscle in Lowry's body tensed. He cleared his throat. "Y-yes, sir," he faltered.

"You hear what we did down at *The Philanthropist* office a couple of months ago?" Bryson asked with quiet pride. A chill rippled at the back of Lowry's neck despite the strong mid-afternoon sunshine. This man must have been part of the mob that ransacked the abolitionist newspaper office and burned down houses in Church Alley. He swallowed hard and did not reply.

"Tell you what, son, if not fer the fact that the road to Walnut Hills is three miles uphill from town and ankle-deep in sticky clay to boot, we'd've burned out that nest of a-bo-litionists at Lane Seminary, too. Yessir, ol' Beecher'd've been in a mess of trouble." He chewed thoughtfully at his cheek. "Seems to me them folks wants to shut down Cincinnati. Don't you know that you can't run a city like this 'thout doin' business with Kentucky? If Kentucky don't have slaves, they can't make no money, and if Kentucky don't have no money, they can't do business in Cincinnati. It's as simple as that."

The bright camaraderie and anticipation of the day vanished. The friendly stagecoach driver clamped his mouth shut and did not say another word to Lowry. When the horses lumbered to a stop at the intersection of Broadway and some other street,

Bryson swung down and spoke earnestly to Father. The next thing Lowry knew, his trunk thumped to the ground and Father, seemingly unmindful of the conflict, popped his head out the window.

"Lowry, our driver says that we pass the road to Lane Seminary on the way to Mr. Chester's house, where I had planned to spend the night. He says Montgomery Pike here will take you straight there, to Gilbert Avenue. It's not far; the driver says it is just around that bend. Can you walk, do you think? It's later than I hoped we would arrive, but this will give you a head start. I would come with you, but Mr. Chester is expecting me." Lowry could see that Father wanted him to go on alone to oblige Bryson.

"I'll walk from here, Father." Lowry watched Bryson's mouth curl into a mean smile. "Good-bye. I'll see you tomorrow." Father gave an encouraging wave and the stagecoach lurched away, leaving Lowry alone in Cincinnati.

What a change! Two days ago, he had been in Ripley, surrounded by his twelve brothers and sisters, Mother, Father, and Amanda. His throat constricted and he vowed not to think of home. The first order of business was to get to Lane Seminary. He swung the trunk to one shoulder and aimed at the curve just ahead.

Bitterly, he remembered the stagecoach driver's remarks about the road to Walnut Hills. The road was a mere shelf carved in the sticky clay of the side hills, pocked by the deep ruts of omnibuses and carriages. Many horses had also cut up the clay with their sharp-shod hooves. Furthermore, Montgomery Pike was liberally covered with road apples, the leavings of many hundreds of horses. Lowry's calves burned as he slogged upward through the mess. He knew why they called them the Walnut *Hills*. Here and there the road leveled a bit, but not for long.

Lowry rounded the curve with eager anticipation. He scanned the surrounding buildings on the tree-lined boulevard. Gradually, it dawned on him that Lane Seminary was nowhere in sight. Once again, he could hear the stagecoach driver as he described why the mob had not burned out Lane Seminary. "The road to Walnut Hills is three miles uphill from town. . . ." He groaned.

By the time Lowry arrived at the seminary, it looked deserted. His legs shook as he stared at the five-story dormitory. He prayed that somebody would be on the first floor, but he reached the top floor before he encountered two young men—seniors, he supposed. When he asked them for help, one of them wordlessly thrust a quilt at him.

Surely, someone at Lane Seminary expected him. He left his trunk and the quilt in an empty room and canvassed the building. A half hour later, he came across the frosty pair of seniors again. He apologized, "I am sorry to bother you again, but can you tell me where to find Dr. Beecher, please?"

"Look here, old friend, a boy has gotten in here among the men and has lost his way," the taller senior sneered to his crony.

"I believe you are right," the other egged him on.

"Seems to me he should go home to his mama. She'll take good care of him."

"Oh, most certainly, most certainly, that is the place for a fresh-faced lad like him," his friend agreed. They snickered and strolled away without a backward glance.

Lowry's face burned. Down the hall, a janitor dragged a broom across the floor, and Lowry raised his voice. "I am a new student. Can you tell me how to get a room here? I thought one was to be ready for me."

"Well, now, I haven't gotten any orders," the janitor replied noncommittally. He jabbed around Lowry's feet with the broom and raised quite a cloud of dust.

Thoroughly discouraged, Lowry trudged back to the dark, cheerless room where he had left his trunk. When he opened the door, the sudden draft rolled tumbleweeds of dust along the floor.

He noticed that the bedstead lacked a mattress. He would spend his first night at the seminary sleeping on the floor. *So much for Christian charity*, he thought dismally. *Small wonder there's a shortage of abolitionist ministers!* At least as a draftsman, he had a warm room—with a bed!—good food, and kind and respectful treatment.

He said his prayers and rolled up in his borrowed quilt. The dust made him sneeze and he squirmed uncomfortably on the dusty floor, but he was so tired and hungry that it made little difference. Just before he fell asleep, he thought, *It has all been a mistake, and I will put it right tomorrow.*

Chapter 10

THE CHEERFUL SUNSHINE mocked him the next morning. The floor had made a hard bed, and his muscles ached from the long walk the previous day. He put himself to rights as best he could and went out into the hall. More students had arrived, along with the superintendent, and Lowry was the last in line. He was so hungry he felt hollow. One by one, the young men departed to their rooms with fresh bedding until only Lowry waited disconsolately.

I should not be here, he thought. *I have made a terrible mistake.* He remembered the seniors and their laughter at his expense and resolved not to go home.

He stepped forward to address the superintendent. "Excuse me, sir, but I must insist upon being assigned a room and bedding. I have been waiting since last night."

The man examined him coldly for three full minutes, as if Lowry were a moth impaled and mounted under glass for display. He wrinkled his nose as his eyes raked Lowry's rumpled clothes, which were grimy with clay and worse. Lowry became acutely aware of the knife-edge pleats in the man's suit, the carefully groomed, glorious head of golden hair, and his immaculate shoes. His face reddened. By comparison, he looked like he had just come from a barn, and he knew he smelled like it, too. Still he held his ground.

"You must address me as Professor King. You are Mr. Rankin, I believe."

"Yes, I am."

"For you, that will be five dollars. In advance," the superintendent demanded coolly, holding out his hand.

"Five dollars?" Lowry stared. "I'm sorry, Professor King, but I cannot advance that amount at this time." He did not say that until he could earn more, he had only ten dollars to his name for both room and board.

"Then we have no room for you."

"Why, how can you say that?" Lowry asked, flabbergasted.

"Quite easily, I assure you. I determine from your politics that you have plenty of cash to spare."

"What do you know of my politics?" Lowry demanded. "I arrived here late yesterday evening, and I expected you to have a room ready for me. Instead, I slept on the floor."

"Ah, yes, last night I had a social engagement." Professor King smiled. "You would have found it very interesting, I assure you. We talked of Cincinnati's increasing commerce, and how it stimulates manufacture."

Lowry wondered if Professor King was right in the head. He had to admit, though, that he had never seen the beat of the business district he had just passed. "But what has that to do with my politics, or how you know what I believe?" He wished he knew what the argument was.

"You will remember to address me as 'sir.'"

Lowry gritted his teeth. "Sir."

"The stimulation of manufacture begs the necessity of trade, you will agree?" the professor went on. "Cincinnati sells the surplus to folks in Kentucky and beyond to make a profit, and we all benefit."

"Yes, if you put it like that, sir." He shifted uneasily.

Professor King drawled, "I don't suppose, Mr. Rankin, that someone like you associates with anyone from Kentucky, though, is that correct?"

Lowry thought of Thomas and Kittie McCague. "Why, of

course I do. Thomas McCague is a good friend of mine, back home in Ripley." He said the name proudly. He knew it would impress Professor King.

The professor took out a pair of gloves and drew them on. "Yes, I thought you knew Mr. McCague. He is the wealthiest man in Ohio, so I've heard tell. Here is an interesting question. How does Thomas McCague make his money?"

Too late, Lowry saw the trap. "I— he ships some pork to Pittsburgh," he stammered.

"Come now, you know he ships most of the pork south, where the plantation owners buy it. They feed slaves with it, did you know that?" the professor purred. "Your friend Mr. McCague has grown wealthy on the backs of slaves, whether you admit it or not."

Deep in his heart, Lowry knew Professor King was right, but he thrust out his lip stubbornly. "Mr. McCague is different. He is a good man."

Professor King smiled and shook his head. He grasped Lowry's arm and steered him to a window. The sweeping view from the fifth floor revealed the Ohio River in the distance, and the Kentucky hills blazed with color just beyond. "You see that, Mr. Rankin? Do you know who lives in Kentucky? My father and mother, whom I love as much as you love your own parents, live across the river, as well as my friends and my business partners. Tell me, should I ignore my friends and relations just because they live a half-mile away, on the other side of the river? Can we help it if we live at the borderline of slavery? They are all good men and women, but I guess you would not associate with them, because they sully their hands with slavery."

"I am happy to live in a free state. Ohio does not trade in slaves." Lowry yanked his arm away. He was convinced now that Professor King was eccentric in the extreme.

Professor King persisted. "Poor young pup," he murmured with pity. "You Ohioans think yourselves so much better than we Kentuckians are. Don't you know that Cincinnati would wither away if she did not trade with slave states?" His voice hardened. "Don't you know that your precious Ohio was the first place in the country to enact Black Laws? Yes, way back in 1804. Since then, Ohio has required every free black or mulatto to produce a court certificate of his actual freedom before he may live here. Then he must register himself and the members of his family with the county clerk's office and pay twelve and a half cents for each. He must do this every two years. Oh, yes, Ohio loves the colored folk," he laughed softly. "Let me tell you about the rest of the black laws."

Lowry did not want to listen any longer. The steward on the *Fair Play*, the stagecoach driver, and now Professor King—he felt as if none of them wanted him here in Cincinnati. They believed they were right about slavery just as deeply as he believed he was right. They went one step further, though, and put teeth behind their beliefs, just what Lowry did not know how to do. They had made the last twenty-four hours mighty uncomfortable for him, and he was ready to give up the fight and leave the seminary forever. He stumbled to the front door and stood on the steps, flustered that he could not better defend his new beliefs. There he stopped in the middle of the stairs and all but blocked the entrance.

"Excuse me, I don't believe we have met." It was a pleasant voice and Lowry was grateful for the friendly greeting. A man who appeared neither old nor young stood before him. He had a broad forehead and large, wide-set smiling eyes, and he beamed at Lowry like the Man in the Moon. His thinning hair contrasted pleasantly with his shaggy eyebrows. He wore his soft, loosely cut clothes as if they were a bothersome necessity; they might have been flour sacks, for all he could tell. He looked bemused yet extremely intelligent. With a cordial nod, the man extended his hand, and Lowry shook it gladly.

"My name is Lowry Rankin, sir; that is, Adam Lowry Rankin, but I'm called Lowry."

"In that case, I'm doubly glad to meet you, Brother Rankin. I am Professor Calvin Stowe. How is your father? And I trust the rest of your family is in good health, as well?" Professor Stowe added as if he really wanted to know. At Lowry's nod, Professor Stowe continued, "Good. I am very glad to see you here, and glad to welcome you to Lane Seminary. I hope you are pleasantly situated?" he inquired solicitously.

A shadow crossed Lowry's face. Reluctantly, he told Professor Stowe his troubles. Thunderclouds gathered on the professor's brow. First, he fumbled in his pocket and withdrew a greasy cloth napkin. He thrust it at Lowry, who unwrapped it, gratefully. It contained a chicken leg and a biscuit, and Lowry thought he had never tasted anything so good.

Next, Professor Stowe swept inside with Lowry in tow. In no time, the superintendent, Professor King, was meekly showing Lowry to a room at Professor Stowe's command. He gave him an empty straw tick while Professor Stowe hovered like a benevolent genie. When Stowe left, however, Professor King did nothing more. "You may take your straw tick to the barn and fill it, if you wish," he shrugged indifferently. Then he left Lowry to the task.

Lowry trudged to the barn and filled the tick with musty straw. He dragged the awkward bundle back to his room, and his face burned as he wrestled with the straw tick and his pride. He tightened the ropes on the decrepit bedstead and flopped the mattress on it. From his pocket, he took a block of wood and three nails, scavenged from a pile of wood scraps in the barn. Taking his own hammer from his trunk, he pounded the nails in a triangle on the block. Just before dark, he placed one of Mother's good beeswax candles into the makeshift holder, where it stood upright, held in place by the nail heads. He scavenged a loan of fire from a neighboring room. Soon candlelight chased the darkness and warmed the corners of the room. Lowry's second night in the seminary seemed a little friendlier with the light and the memory of his advocate, Professor Stowe.

"Father, I couldn't defend what I believe. I even found myself wondering whether I was in the wrong. It is enough to make me reconsider whether God has called me to this ministry," Lowry confided the next morning. He and Father sat on the bed and ate the warm doughnuts Mrs. Chester had sent.

Father chose his words carefully before speaking. "I have seen Professor Stowe, Lowry. He assures me that you belong here. The superintendent is pro-slavery, and he has had ample time to think up responses to some of the best arguments in the country against slavery, as advanced by Mr. Weld in the Lane debates. He also knows that I supported the Lane students who protested and left the school."

Lowry studied his father. If it bothered him that men did not like him because of his position on slavery, he did not show it. He had never seen Father at a loss for words. How did he always know exactly what to say?

"Lowry," Father advised now, "you must treat the superintendent with respect. Although he does not share your views, he is a part of the faculty. I have no doubt that the Lord will sustain you and uphold you. Depend on Him as the lions roar about you and He will preserve you from harm, just as He protected Daniel in the lions' den."

His courage bolstered, Lowry escorted Father to the door. Then he squared his shoulders. *Let the lions do their worst*, he thought. He returned to the seminary, determined to stay for the duration.

Later that afternoon, the lions Father had spoken of lunged

for Lowry's throat. Professor King sent a note demanding Lowry's attendance at an examination to determine which students should enter the junior class. Lowry was embarrassed. He meant to read and study under Drs. Beecher and Stowe for the first year, to determine what he lacked in his education, and then to make a fresh start next year. Nonetheless, the note definitely commanded him to be present and prepared for examination. He spent a sleepless night wondering how he would present his case.

The next morning, his knees knocked and he sat down quickly at the back of the platform in the junior lecture room. He skulked behind the other nine candidates and tried to think what he should say when his turn came. He hoped it would not come soon. Professor King led the prayer, and to Lowry's relief, Dr. Beecher himself entered the room and addressed the candidates. He spoke about the importance and grandeur of Christian ministry, and Lowry felt all his doubts wash away as the welcome words bolstered his soul. He relaxed for the first time since his arrival at Lane.

"Mr. Rankin! You will come and give us an account of your Christian experience, and your reason or motive for entering the Christian ministry." Professor King fixed him with a steely gaze.

It seemed an age until his legs would support him. He walked mechanically to the pulpit and gripped the edges, his mouth like cotton. The members of the learned faculty stared solemnly at him, just as the elders had when Lowry had joined the church so long ago. Only Professor Stowe nodded encouragement.

"I—I did not intend, that is, I do not wish to enter the class at this time," he stammered, but that was not what he had planned to say at all. "I mean to say, I understood that my first year could be a sort of—a trial, so's I could study a spell." He nearly groaned aloud. What a time for his accent to return! He gulped and tried again. "I mean study for a while, to see whether . . ." he trailed off into wretched silence. He could see Professor King's sly smile in the shadows. He shook his great curly head of hair and looked as pleased as a farm cat with a sleek brown mouse trapped under its sharp claws. Out of the corner of his eye, Lowry observed Professor Stowe lean to make a remark to his father-in-law, Dr. Beecher, and both men rocked in silent mirth. Could they be laughing at him? He felt betrayed and utterly alone.

"That is well," Lowry heard Professor King say, "and it is very wise for a young person to follow a trial plan. Unfortunately, we have no such course here at Lane Seminary. Only the most serious of applicants may be considered. I am sure you can understand our position," he purred. "Perhaps it would be best if your father helps you at home."

Professor Stowe interrupted. "Brother Rankin has come to Lane because of the superior advantages of our seminary course over what he can glean at home. I see no harm from his pursuing such a course for a year."

Lowry glanced uneasily at Professor King, who glowered at Professor Stowe. Then Dr. Beecher added fuel to the fire. "That is well put!"

Suddenly Lowry was angry. He had no desire to cause an awkward rift among the members of the faculty. His spine stiffened and he leaned forward on his elbows to fix Professor King with a gaze free of fear. He spoke in a clear, quiet voice. "In order to relieve the faculty of any embarrassment caused by a difference of opinion on my account, I will be a candidate for membership in the junior class. I will study hard if I am allowed to enter. You may administer your examination now."

Several men gasped. After a rigorous question-and-answer session, Lowry triumphed; the entire group sustained his candidacy, and he retired from the floor covered in glory.

At noon, he stood outside Dr. Beecher's office, at the president's request. He heard a fiddle squawk as somebody scraped out a wheezy rendition of "Auld Lang Syne." How could Dr. Beecher put up with such a racket? He knocked on the door.

"Yes?" Dr. Beecher himself peeped out with a befuddled expression, but he possessed a commanding presence, nevertheless. A pair of bow spectacles perched on his prominent, distinguished nose, and he had a pronounced widow's peak. Dramatic swoops of gray fanned out through his dark hair at the temples, and the corners of his mouth turned down. Then Dr. Beecher smiled. His face became fatherly and kind.

"I'm Lowry Rankin, sir. I have an appointment with you."

"Oh, heavens to Betsy, yes, you do! Come in, come in! Just let me put away my fiddle." He peered around the room; although a fiddle case lay in plain sight on a chair, he took no notice. Inside it sat a man's hat, presumably Dr. Beecher's. Lowry smiled inwardly. "I play the fiddle to relax myself when I am overwrought," Dr. Beecher continued. "I can't think where I have mislaid the—how do you call it—the—the box I keep it in." He waved the instrument vaguely and laid it across a hat rack.

"Well, Brother Rankin, congratulations!" Dr. Beecher shook his hand. "Your excellent examination results allow you to enter the junior class after all, to the consternation of some." The president of Lane Seminary had a very undignified twinkle in his eye. "You know, Brother Rankin, Professor King said afterward that he did not expect you to succeed. I fear 'twas simply because you are an abolitionist. Remember, he is for slavery as much as you are against it."

"I am becoming very aware of the risks involved in being an abolitionist, Dr. Beecher," Lowry assured him.

"Well, if you want to speak of risks, you are here after the fireworks, young man. You should have been here two months ago, when that printing press mob was bent on burning out every abolitionist in town!"

Lowry started. *So Dr. Beecher knew he was in danger that night!* The stagecoach driver had told the truth.

Dr. Beecher unhooked the bows of his spectacles from his ears and polished the glass with his handkerchief. He picked his teeth thoughtfully with the earpiece and spoke again. "That was one night when defense was more than just a matter of fancy words. Thank the good Lord that nothing came of it. But we were ready, nonetheless." The man wiped his face with the same dainty, flowered handkerchief. "Only my son Henry Ward, my son-in-law Professor Stowe, and a handful of students were here that night. I told them that they had the right of self-defense, that they could arm themselves, and if the mob came, they could shoot." He looked left, then right, pulled a wry face, and stage-whispered behind his hand, "But I told them not to kill 'em. I told them, 'Aim low; hit 'em in the legs! Hit 'em in the legs!'"

Fascinated, Lowry stared at Dr. Beecher for one long minute. Then he and the minister shared a hearty laugh that did Lowry a world of good. "I wish I could think that clearly under pressure," Lowry said. "I never know what to say, or how to defend my position. In the past days, I must admit I have wondered whether I am qualified to be a minister." His voice shook.

"Hogwash!" Dr. Beecher waved his hand. "Brother Rankin, you were not at a loss for words this morning. You'll make a fine abolition minister. Just you remember who's in charge." He winked and pointed toward the ceiling. "I'll let you in on a secret. God Almighty runs this world, not Professor King. Good day, and I extend my heartiest congratulations!"

A great weight rolled from Lowry's shoulders. Overwhelmed with gratitude, he turned to go, but he stopped.

"Dr. Beecher?"

"Yes, Brother Rankin?"

"There's just one more thing. I believe I saw Professor Stowe make a private remark to you, just as Professor King prepared to speak. You laughed together. Was it because of the way I talk?"

Dr. Beecher frowned. "I am sorry, Brother Rankin." He shook

his head. "No, my son-in-law merely reported an impression of Professor King that he had heard from the students. Perhaps he was uncouth to relate it at such a serious time." Dr. Beecher's tone was solemn, but his lips twitched in the direction of a smile.

"Thank you, sir, for telling me. Think nothing of it."

Dr. Beecher cleared his throat and smothered a chuckle. He spoke in a low voice, his face wreathed in a gentle smile.

"He said, 'See the lion shake his mane!'"

Lowry grinned at Dr. Beecher and strolled from the office with his hands in his pockets. He whistled "Auld Lang Syne," and before he had gone many steps, the caterwauling fiddle joined the serenade.

Lowry had barely settled down to his studies that afternoon when he received another note, a summons to report to the Anti-Slavery Office in Cincinnati immediately. His heart thudded—perhaps Father had been attacked by a pro-slavery mob! He dashed down the dormitory stairs and broke into a trot. At least the slimy road was downhill all the way to town. The late afternoon sun slanted across the road before he ducked down an alley and entered the office.

"Rankin?" questioned a man briefly. He stood behind a high counter covered with papers.

"Yes, sir."

"Good. There is not a moment to lose." The man lowered his voice. "A fugitive is hidden among the colored people here. Already several parties are seeking him. His master has offered a five hundred dollar reward for his return." He wasted no time on unnecessary details.

Anxiety for Father's safety shifted to fear for the hunted man. The lure of five hundred dollars caused men to do ugly things. "He is in real trouble," Lowry said slowly.

"Yes, the matter is most urgent. The river patrol is searching every house. It is only a matter of time until they find him, unless—"

The agent paused, and Lowry waited, not understanding.

"That is, your father led me to believe—"

And then Lowry knew. Father had told the agent to send for good old dependable Lowry Rankin.

"Is there no one else?" *Confound Father!* Lowry rubbed his forehead and thought of Professor King. If he found Lowry absent from his studies after his solemn promise to work hard, the superintendent would never let the matter rest.

"I'm sorry, Rankin, there's not," the man said with real regret.

"Who keeps the next station?" Lowry sighed. Perhaps he could return before anyone noticed his absence.

"A Quaker, William Butterworth," the man answered shortly.

"Butterworth?"

"He lives twenty-five miles north of here. The fugitive's life is in grave danger. He needs to be far from Cincinnati as quickly as possible."

Lowry gaped at the agent. "Twenty-five miles! It's late afternoon!" He scowled and ran a hand through his hair. The fugitive desperately needed help. He narrowed his eyes. "I need a good team and a carriage with curtains."

The man gave him a shrewd glance. "You mean a Liberator? Very well."

Lowry had never heard the term in his life, but he caught on quickly and nodded. "I need clear directions—I'm not familiar with the country, so I need a good lantern, too. Now, where do I find him?" he finished.

Clearly impressed, the agent answered, "Well, Mr. Rankin, you'll have your team, your directions, and our thanks. Start down at Church Alley." He lowered his voice still more. "If I were you, I'd run without a light until I was well out of town."

By eight o'clock, with the fugitive safely hidden in the Liberator after a long search, Lowry left Cincinnati and headed north. The horses struck out willingly after a hearty feed and a cool drink. Lowry had missed his own supper, and he was so hungry that he thought he might relish a feedbag. "Go ahead and growl," he grimly addressed his stomach, "this one missed meal will not amount to much." He concentrated on the small starburst of light cast on the road by the swinging lantern. Ghostly gray moths blundered about the glass, and once Lowry almost jumped out of his skin when a nighthawk swooped low at them, its hungry mouth agape. The sway of the carriage lulled him; he was tired down to his bones. How long ago this morning and his examination seemed! He fought to stay awake and watched for his landmarks as the weary miles rolled by.

The rest of the trip passed in a dream. He scarcely realized he had returned to the livery stable until the horses nickered softly, delighted to be home after the fifty-mile round trip. Then the hostler slapped the horses' dusty rumps good-naturedly, rubbed noses that nuzzled for a treat. He touched his cap to Lowry; the nightmare was almost over.

Lowry staggered toward Walnut Hills. A glimmer of golden light gilded the horizon. He would have to leg it to reach his bunk before anyone else was astir. Try as he might, however, he managed only a brisk walk that nonetheless whittled away the remaining two miles to the seminary.

A half hour later, famished, cold, and bone-tired, Lowry crawled quietly into his bed. One more man lived in freedom because of his night's work, but Lane Seminary slumbered on, unaware.

Gratefully Lowry clutched the covers to his chin. Immediately sleep descended and he sank blissfully down, down—

"Up and at 'em, Brother Rankin!" A hearty voice jarred him back to life. His neighbor jangled, "You going lazy on us? It's already five past six!"

Lowry groaned inwardly. He rubbed his face and rolled out of bed, asleep on his feet. He remembered his solemn promise to

God and despaired. He would never graduate from Lane Seminary and become an abolitionist minister if he spent most of his nights aiding fugitives.

Chapter 11

WITH EVERY FIBER OF HIS BEING, Lowry wished to be home in Ripley. He lay on the musty straw tick, Mother's letter dangling from his listless fingers. It was April, and the news of Father's condition had finally reached Lane Seminary. His cough had worsened until he could scarcely breathe. Father had returned early from an antislavery campaign, so Lowry knew he was dangerously ill. Probably consumption, Mother warned, and it remained uncertain whether Father would pull through.

Worried as he was, Lowry could not help smiling a little. Whenever he was ill, Father dourly predicted that consumption would be the death of him. Lowry argued that if anyone had ruined his health with countless trips in the unhealthy night air, *he* had, and he would die of consumption before Father succumbed.

Life at Lane Seminary had taken a heavy toll on Lowry, physically, mentally, and spiritually. The one hundred or so slaves he had transported northward since October, sometimes as far as sixty-five miles one way; the constant battle of wits with Professor King, who fouled up the job that should have provided Lowry's board; and the regular classes and odd moments of study left him little time to read his Bible. Because he had no money, he'd found a job stripping seed from broomcorn for a local farmer, who had paid him in potatoes. There had been an awful eight-week stretch when he had lived on nothing but saltwater and potatoes, but he had not borrowed money. After that, a broom factory set up in the basement of his dormitory. He was the first to hire on, even though stripping seed again nearly drove him to distraction, because the dust made his skin itch like fire. Nevertheless, he desperately needed the three cents he made on each broom he completed. He could make fifteen brooms in three hours, which equated to forty-five cents a day. With this second job, he could support himself, but now he was spread even thinner.

The letter slipped to the floor as a hard cough shook his whole body. He tried to sit up. The room swam before his eyes. Lowry knew he was ill. Never had he felt so alone and helpless. His head throbbed and his skin felt papery. He longed for a cool drink, but instead he dozed, unaware of the passage of time. He fell into a fitful sleep as he asked God that Father's health should be restored.

"Brother Rankin? Brother Rankin?"

In his fevered dreams, a still, small voice called him relentlessly. His hands moved as if to wave it away.

"Brother Rankin!" the voice insisted hollowly. "Brother Rankin! Wake up, Brother Rankin!"

Lowry stared dully. Something moved. He turned his head to follow the movement, but how it hurt!

"Please, Brother Rankin!" The room swam into focus, and he saw a black face. "They sent me here. My master's coming after me. The freedmen done told me you would help. Please wake up!" Desperation caused the man's voice to shake.

Lowry tried to clear his head as thoughts chased around and around. A desperate refugee had been sent to him for help. The situation was perilous. It was too late to wonder why the man had been sent directly to him—here he stood, in grave danger. To keep the man on the premises until Lowry recovered was out of the question; he must be moved to the next station immediately. But how, without a carriage, or even a horse? The sky was already pearly gray. Walking to safety before daylight would not be possible, even if Lowry were in the pink of health. To be seen after daylight in the company of a fugitive meant certain arrest.

Another deep, congested cough nearly bent him double, and flakes of dried skin showered from his parched lips.

Lowry shivered miserably in his thin nightclothes. He could not do it. He stared dejectedly at the runaway and the distraught man mirrored his mood, undoubtedly coming to the same disheartening conclusion as Lowry.

"Brother Rankin, you're feeling poorly. I'm right sorry to trouble you. Reckon I'll push on by myself. I'll get by," the man mumbled.

Lowry was sorely tempted to let the man go on alone, but doubt niggled at his feverish thoughts. If only he had a friend here in Cincinnati! Someone upon whom he could depend utterly, someone—

Then Lowry thought he knew just the person. He swayed to his feet and gingerly pulled on his clothes.

"Come with me," Lowry whispered, and his head seemed to whirl. The black man silently obeyed.

Lowry reeled through the back alleys in the early April chill. The slave stuck closer than a shadow, practically clutching Lowry's sleeve to keep track of him in the gloom under the trees. Was he wrong to go to his teacher, Professor Stowe? Brilliant, bright-eyed, and kind, the professor had proven a worthy ally when Lowry desperately needed one. Now he had no choice.

Lowry staggered to the Stowes' house in Walnut Hills and hid the fugitive in the barn. Before he knew it, he was in the kitchen, pouring out his predicament in a whisper to his kind-hearted teacher. When he finished, he lowered his head to the tabletop, which was covered with sheaves of brown wrapping paper, liberally scribbled. His head throbbed as he waited.

"Well, I must say, Brother Rankin, that you have shouldered more than your share of hardship in your short time at Lane. What to do, what to do?" Dr. Stowe steepled his fingertips. "The runaway must be sent along, but how?" His bushy eyebrows puckered.

"Well, Brother Rankin, one thing is certain. You cannot be out in the night air. It is far too damp for a man as unwell as you are." He paused and rubbed his chin. "However, it is equally true that you cannot keep the poor fellow in safety this close to the city." The professor stopped, the logic of the problem beyond his reckoning.

"What can I do," Lowry moaned, "but venture the going afoot? The risk would be the less. I might not be disturbed early this morning if I kept to the woods. We'll have to wade the Miami."

Professor Stowe blanched. "That icy water! You have a fever! No, Brother Rankin, you must not do that." Dimly Lowry wondered if Professor Stowe was as squeamish about illness as he was.

Lowry hesitated. "Might you loan me your carriage? I think I can manage to drive."

Professor Stowe brightened. "Why, Brother Rankin, I don't know why I didn't think of it before. Of course, it is the only way. Certainly!" he nodded vehemently.

"Then you'll let me borrow your carriage and horse?" Lowry's legs trembled as he leaned heavily on the table and tried to stand. His hand skidded on the piles of brown paper and they skittered to the floor. Professor Stowe picked up the papers one at a time.

"My wife's a writer," he confided. A fond smile lingered on his lips as he stacked the scribbled papers lovingly. "Her stories appear in the newspapers." He seemed to have forgotten Lowry was there.

"Your horse and carriage? You'll loan them to me?" Lowry pressed.

"Why, of course not. Don't you see?" Professor Stowe said earnestly. "The only way out of your difficulty is for *me* to take my horse and carriage and convey the refugee *myself*!"

Lowry stared at his friend, dumbfounded. People rightly described Professor Stowe as a genius, no doubt about that, but his vagueness worried Lowry. Sometimes he seemed almost child-like as he pottered about in a bewildered daze. He wondered whether he should entrust a man's life to someone as scatter-brained as Professor Stowe.

He rubbed his aching forehead and focused on the man with difficulty. Their eyes met and held, and Lowry saw steadfastness there, a willingness to try. *With God's help*, the professor seemed to say, *I can do it.*

"Professor Stowe—" Lowry began gratefully, but the professor held up his hand.

"Tut, tut, someone else can teach my classes today, and my wife will only think I am at school. I will vouch that you were too unwell to attend. Now, what shall I do?" The professor asked briskly, much as he would in the classroom.

Patiently and carefully, Lowry described in detail the way to William Butterworth's farm, hesitating only when his dulled mind came to the river. The ford was extremely tricky even for an experienced traveler.

"You see, sir, the ford is crooked. Any more rain will raise the water, but not enough to endanger crossing if you follow my instructions exactly," Lowry cautioned.

"You may be sure that I will turn neither to the right nor to the left, Brother Rankin. 'Straight is the gate, and narrow is the way which leadeth unto life, and few there be that find it,' eh?" Professor Stowe quoted from the Bible with a twinkle in his eye. He seemed to enjoy the prospect of the adventure immensely. Lowry could only manage a wan smile in return.

A short while later, the professor jiggled the reins over his horse's back. He waved good-bye, his moon-face beaming. With the fugitive safely hidden in the carriage, Lowry's spirits rose from forlorn despair to glimmering hope. He asked God to protect his friend. Then he staggered off to the warm, dim, fragrant hay-loft to doze until his fearful headache and fever subsided.

Light flickered on Lowry's eyelids and he awoke with a start. A long rumble of thunder growled and echoed in the distance; he could feel the reverberations to his very core. The smell of rain wafted through the rafters and he thought of Mother, how she enjoyed the cleansing rains of springtime. He missed his family with a keen pain, sharpened by his illness and ill treatment. Nothing had worked out since the day he'd made his vow to fight human slavery. When he'd come to Cincinnati last fall, there had been a lift to his chin and determination in his step. Now his shoulders drooped and he had difficulty looking other men in the eye. He remembered his brave words and misery engulfed him. "I pray God I may never be persuaded to give up the fight until slavery is dead or the Lord calls me home," he whispered. The countless midnight trips to transport fugitives during his time at Lane had cost him nearly every ounce of his health and strength, and consumed his study time. He was no nearer to being an abolitionist minister than he'd been last fall. "I am ready to give up, Lord," he prayed. "I can't do it."

In the stillness, he heard a whisper, then another, like the hushed murmur of a congregation before the church service begins. He strained his ears as the sound changed to the liquid plunk of a handful of pebbles tossed into a creek. A cool drop of water splashed on his forehead, and the heavens opened and crashed on the barn roof with a roar. He rolled to a more sheltered spot under the eaves. He breathed deeply, unable to get enough of the cool, rain-sweetened air on his hot face. Gradually the rain on the roof slowed to a patter, and Lowry thought drowsily of Amanda Kephart. He could feel her white hand cool on his forehead. Her eyes, as blue as a deep blue September sky, were filled with tenderness as she cared for him. He smiled and dozed.

A barn swallow swooped low past his ear on her way to her nest. Lowry awoke and stared in dismay. The light had a late-day look, and Amanda was not there, after all. His heart ached. She had been right there beside him, so real, but he must have dreamed it. In that telltale instant, Lowry knew that he loved her. He meant to tell her so, the minute he got back home.

The grate of wood on gravel roused him. He could barely make out the dim outlines of the Stowes' barn. Now he remembered where he was, and why. Had Professor Stowe succeeded? He heard the telltale rattle of a carriage wheel. Groggily, he slipped among the shadows to await his friend's return. He brushed hay from his clothes. In the half-light, he saw the professor's horse and carriage come to a stop and he hurried forward to help unhitch.

"I'm relieved you have returned." Lowry reached to help Professor Stowe alight. "But—what's this?" he asked as he steadied the professor's shoulder. "Your coat is soaked!" He ran his hand over the carriage cushions. They felt squashy and damp. In alarm, he blurted, "What happened, sir? How come you're all wet?"

Professor Stowe laughed good-naturedly. "Brother Rankin, if it had not been for the efficient help of your colored friend, Lane Seminary would have had one less professor today!" He paused as if he did not quite believe his statement himself. "Just think of your having been the occasion of my death," he mused, struck by the novelty of the thought.

Lowry's knees buckled and he sat down weakly on the carriage step, his face drained of color. "What happened?" he whispered.

"No harm done, Brother Rankin. The night has grown quite warm, and I've suffered no ill. Don't worry, no one will be able to say that a Lane Seminary professor was drowned 'stealing slaves.' Why," he digressed, "if the Cincinnati rabble got wind of such a thing, not one of the seminary buildings would remain standing. Well, I am glad I got only a good ducking. Also, that I got the poor fellow safely to the station."

Lowry breathed a small sigh of thanks as Professor Stowe mopped his damp brow with a handkerchief and took up his story afresh.

"You were right, Brother Rankin, that was a tricky ford! Apparently, I did not keep to the river long enough, but turned too soon. The river was a good deal swollen in volume by the rain and I found my horse was suddenly plunged into deep water with the current carrying us downstream." Professor Stowe might have been talking about someone else's experience rather than his own.

The rain—he had forgotten! Lowry closed his eyes and dreaded to hear more. He could imagine the swift, coffee-with-cream colored water as it foamed around the closed carriage, and the balky horse as it trembled and snorted. Vividly, one more picture flashed through his mind. He saw Professor Stowe's trusting, cheerful round face as he clucked encouragement to his horse and urged him innocently into the rushing water at the wrong ford. Lowry's eyes popped open. With a shaky hand, he blotted cold sweat from his forehead.

"As the water surged up around me, I heard a heavy splash. The water came up to my neck and I couldn't see anything, and the carriage bounced about like a cork in the river. I came near being drowned. You see," he added, "I cannot swim any better than a pebble!"

Lowry gulped. Professor Stowe warmed to the story.

"Then I saw the colored man. He is a fine swimmer. He angled to one side of my horse, which plunged frightfully, and grabbed the bit. 'Ho, ho, fellow,' he said, and as the horse quieted, he started him swimming. We reached shallow water and your man led us safely to the bank, then up to the crossing. On the further side we had no mishap, and reached the station all right—except for the drenching!" Professor Stowe tilted his head and smiled. "Brother Rankin, I may well be the only minister of my denomination who ever was baptized by immersion," he chuckled.

Lowry smiled feebly. Professor Stowe pressed heedlessly on. He did not seem to notice his pupil's distress.

"Friend Butterworth and family were anxious that I should stay until morning and dry my clothes, but as the river was rising rapidly, I preferred to come back at once. Butterworth accompanied me on horseback, to guide me to the proper ford. We crossed safely though the water was considerably higher than before. After seeing my guide cross back over the river unharmed, I returned here—as you see."

Praise God, thought Lowry fervently.

"Now, my brother," resumed Professor Stowe, "I think you had better do all the fording of that river without me. Say nothing about how near I came to drowning and no one need be the wiser." After pausing, he added, "Especially, there is no need for Mrs. Stowe to know." For a moment, he was startlingly lucid.

"No need for me to know what, Cal?"

Lowry thought his heart would stop. A tiny woman peered curiously around the side of the carriage; her corkscrew curls danced. She had large, clear gray eyes and—most regrettably for a woman—Dr. Beecher's prominent nose. This must be Mrs. Stowe, who was Lyman Beecher's daughter and Calvin Stowe's wife. Already Lowry suspected that Father, who had warned him many years ago never to speak outside the family about the fugitives he aided, would not have asked Professor Stowe for help, no matter what the circumstances. He must not risk taking yet another person into his confidence, especially one who wrote stories for the newspapers. He gave a low moan and hacked until he thought his eyeballs would drop from his head.

"Why, you're really ill!" the tiny woman exclaimed. "Cal, what's wrong with him? He doesn't have the cholera, does he?" Fear lingered behind her words. "Is that what you thought I didn't need to know?"

"My dear, this is one of my students, Lowry Rankin. His father—"

"Why, I know his father very well, if he is John Rankin! He's a fine man. I won't soon forget the first time I heard him speak. I've known him longer than I have known you, Cal, if it comes to that. Yes, indeed, he is quite handsome, too. But what's the matter?"

"I'm afraid it's a bronchial sore throat, ma'am. I have a fever and a cough," Lowry said.

She touched his forehead. "Why, you're burning up! Cal, help him to bed. I'll send Zillah for some things, and make up some good, health-giving soup, and take care of him."

"Really, ma'am, there's no need." Lowry felt guilty. He had only meant to divert her attention, not impose on her kindness. But the thought of hot soup and a warm bed sounded nice. He vowed to help her when he felt better; a good night's sleep should work wonders. Perhaps then he could chop some wood or repair a fence. He followed the unsuspecting woman to the house as her husband slunk behind. She was so preoccupied as she fussed over Lowry that she did not notice that Professor Stowe's surtout dripped and his shoes squelched.

Lowry sank gratefully into the snowy drift of a feather tick and snuggled under the bright counterpane. He barely roused himself to sip the hot broth that Mrs. Stowe spooned into his mouth, but oh it tasted so good and eased the pain in his throat, as well. He drank it down and nestled into the soft bed with a sigh. Mrs. Stowe sat beside him with her head bowed. The yellow candlelight cast a soft halo around her hair and glowed in the thousand crinkles that waved over her neck. Professor Stowe reappeared and told Lowry not to worry one particle about anything.

If only it were that easy! The doubts that had threatened to overwhelm him as he waited in the barn crept back as soon as his friends left the room. He turned toward the wall to shut out the accusing voices in his mind that told him he had failed.

Eventually, he fell asleep, but it was a troubled sleep. His misery spilled over into his dreams.

He dreamed he saw Sherwood, happy as a lark, skipping down the path with a cane fishing pole over his shoulder. The boy beckoned with a touch of his old carefree fire, and Lowry dashed to join him. But before he could reach his old friend, a pair of dead white hands snatched Sherwood and dragged him into the bushes. "Sherwood, no!" Lowry screamed, but no sound came from his mouth, and he could not move to help his friend.

The scene changed and Lowry dreamed he rode Old Sorrel through the woods at midnight. He had a full sack of flour slung over his back—he thought this strange, because he had never carried flour home from the mill that way before. What was more, the sack writhed and squirmed. As Lowry and Old Sorrel passed under the darkest of trees, the sack popped open and Tice's David stuck out his head. Lowry screamed again, but still there was no sound. He struggled to push David back into the sack, but the grinning head stayed right there, hooked over Lowry's shoulder. "David! You have to hide! You have to hide! They'll catch you and sell you down the river!" Lowry sobbed over and over.

Mercifully, the dream changed again, and Lowry relaxed. He was on a steamboat excursion; the sun glinted gently on the Ohio River, and somehow he knew that Amanda waited for him at the end of his journey. He walked with Father to get his trunk. Then Father shook his hand, but, strange to say, he would not look Lowry in the eye. At least, he knew that everything would be all right when he met Amanda. He loaded his trunk onto the top of a shiny, black stagecoach and took his seat beside the driver. The man shook the reins and they rattled. Lowry saw that the horses were hitched with long chains instead of leather harnesses and reins.

"Will you help me?" the driver asked. "I can't whip that near leader. You do it for me." He thrust the whip into Lowry's hands, though he did not want to take it. He raised the whip and looked at the front horse on the left side, but there was no horse. Instead, he saw Amanda, dressed in her prettiest pink dress, chained with the rest of the beasts, and her blue eyes were dark with fear as she implored him to have mercy.

He could not breathe, and sweat poured off him. He flung himself down to unhitch her, but the driver's strong hands held him back. "I have to help Amanda!" he cried. "She is a slave! I have to get her away from here!" He could not move, and his throat ached with the force of his screams.

He thrashed wildly against the cruel hands that held him. "Lowry! Lowry!" he heard. "You're all right!" Dimly he realized that someone held him and sobbed, but it was not the driver. He shook his head, opened his eyes, and looked into Mrs. Stowe's tear-stained face.

"Thank God! Thank God!" she breathed. "I am at the end of my strength."

Unable to recall where he was, or why his teacher's wife held his wrists, or why he was soaked with sweat, Lowry tried to sit up—and then he knew. He was out of his head with fever, and the Stowes had taken him under wing. Mrs. Stowe caught her breath and sat down in a rush-bottomed chair. She looked at him very oddly.

Lowry sank weakly to the pillow. His head ached, his throat ached, and it seemed even his bones ached. He croaked hoarsely and Mrs. Stowe held a cool dipper of water to his lips.

"Such a turn you gave us," she murmured. "I sent the professor for a physician. They should be here shortly." She started to say something more, but instead she pressed her fingers to her lips, as if to hold back her words. She rested her arm on the back of her chair and supported her chin. Her eyes grew large as she stared out the window at the black walnut grove that towered over the house and barn. "Lowry?" Her voice was thin and far away, even though she sat next to him. "Who is Sherwood?"

He froze. Several long seconds slipped past. His shirtfront moved with an almost imperceptible lift from his slamming heart. How much had he given away while his fever raged?

"A friend," he rasped cautiously.

"Very well," Mrs. Stowe said slowly. "Sometimes the unconscious mind reveals what we do not wish to share." She tucked in the counterpane. "Rest now. I have something to confide, and you shall judge whether you can trust me." She tipped some water from a china pitcher decorated with violets into a matching washbasin, then wrung out a cloth and sponged his hot face before she continued. "Nigh on four years ago, I visited Mr.—no, I shall not tell you his name, for you may know of him. It's enough to say that I visited a plantation in Kentucky. I attended a slave auction."

If Lowry had not been drained of energy, he would have reacted. Instead, he lay very still as her words wrapped around him and revived all the ghastly memories he had tried to forget. "I saw slaves—members of the same family—chained, cruelly whipped, and sold away from one another. I saw a wife never again to embrace her husband, a child never again to receive a tender kiss from his loving mother. Death alone can separate me from my family, but to live, and to lose so much!" A tear splashed on her lace fichu. She blotted her eyes with a handkerchief and twisted it in her slender hands. "Screams and sobs such as I never wish to hear again, that I cannot stop from piercing me through, that is what I heard that dreadful day. Such scenes affect me deeply; they sink into my heart and mind until a simple word triggers the memory, and then I see the horror again, right before me. And, oh, Lowry," she breathed, "you have seen it, too!"

Lowry felt the blood drain from his face, and he shivered until his teeth chattered. Mrs. Stowe did not notice. "Yet I sense a difference. Somehow, you have something to do with the Underground that I've heard tell of. You have helped Sherwood and David, and many more, I suspect. Now, there," she hushed his protests. "You needn't answer. Still, I wonder, what can *I* do?" she whispered, as tears streamed down her cheeks. "I am only a woman. What can *I* do against slavery? Oh, Lowry, I envy you so!"

He was shocked. *Envy? How could she possibly envy me?* he wondered in his fever-dulled state. Perhaps she knew he aimed to be an abolition minister, like Lyman Beecher, her famous father, and Henry Ward Beecher, her brother. Women were not allowed to enter the ministry, so she could never be like them. He felt like a mean, low sneak to think how disappointed she would be if she knew how far short he was of that goal.

Then his heart filled with pity as he remembered her agony over the slave auction. He wanted to reassure her that Father had seen the necessity, long ago, of providing a way to help refugees, but it was not his secret to tell. He risked financial ruin and prison for the Rankins if he divulged his family's business. Too many innocent lives depended on his silence.

"Well, Hattie, is the patient with us still? I've fetched the doctor." Calvin Stowe stood on the threshold of the room. Mrs. Stowe dabbed her wet cheeks with the twisted bit of lace and her great gray eyes burned through Lowry. He knew then that she would never betray him.

"We have had a rough time, but I believe we have seen a light at the end of the tunnel." Her steady gaze never left his face. She had mentioned envy, and he could see it nearly consumed her, but for the life of him, he could not imagine why she envied a miserable failure like him.

While the doctor fussed over Lowry, the doubts that had twice assailed him today overwhelmed him again. It all seemed so hopeless. He needed to study hard to be a successful abolition minister, so he could one day preach that God desired slaves to be free. Yet, there were slaves who desired to be free now, and their transport took away Lowry's study time, and many nights of his sleep, too. When he tried to do everything at once, he became so ill he could do nothing. The whole year had been a waste of everyone's time. He hung his head.

"Professor Stowe?" he mumbled. "I am not fit to be a minister. I think . . . I want to go home to Ripley."

Chapter 12

Hot puffs of wind raced northward across the Eminence. The steamy air swirled sluggishly, rattling the dry leaves but offering little relief from the heat. Lowry watched the clouds blossom upward like bright white explosions of popcorn in the merciless afternoon sun. Now and then, a shadow winged across the golden Kentucky fields on the opposite side of the Ohio as sullen, darker clouds sailed east on higher, faster currents.

A faint keening reached Lowry's ears and he saw a tiny speck that spiraled high overhead. He watched the red-tailed hawk ride the rising warm air until it disappeared from view, and he shook his head. The young people of Ripley were looking forward eagerly to the Brown County Music Convention the next day at Sardinia, where Ludovicus Weld would hold a singing school. The conventioneers looked in a fair way to get wet as they traveled, but no one wanted to miss the fun because of a little rain. They had arranged to drive the twenty miles in a procession of carriages, and Lowry meant to escort Amanda. He had something important to ask her, away from all his brothers and sisters, and away from hers, as well.

The only thing that had sustained him through his long bout of bronchial pneumonia and slow recovery was the thought that he would see Amanda again. Before the Stowes had sent him home to Ripley, they had argued with a vehemence worthy of Father's that Lowry should stay the course. It was no use. He had made up his mind to leave the seminary, become a carpenter, and marry Amanda, in that order. That is, if she would have him.

Summer work on the farm had kept him so busy that they had not had a chance to talk in private. A casual nod in the street or at church was all he could manage. Now it was September; he had waited long enough.

The rest of the family sat soberly at the table while Lowry washed his hands and face at the tin basin outside. Father asked the blessing. Lowry noticed the many unhappy faces that avoided his gaze. He wondered what could be the matter now, but he refused to let their mood spoil his anticipation.

Father and Mother looked at him. The rest of the family silently concentrated on their plates. Gently, Mother began, "Lowry, I'm sorry . . ." but her voice faded.

Father asked bluntly, "Lowry, who will take care of the fugitives who come this weekend, if you older boys all go off to Sardinia?"

The air hummed as they all awaited Lowry's answer. His anger flared white-hot as he stared at Father.

So that's the trouble! Slaves intruded into every corner of Lowry's life, and sure enough, some poor wretch might need his help, just when his own future beckoned. He waged a heated battle with his uncharitable thoughts as the other boys looked on anxiously.

His anger died, though, when he thought of Amanda, how she never complained, and of Mrs. Stowe's anguish over the plight of the slaves. *One last time*, he told himself. Lowry heard himself saying slowly, "I will stay home, Father, if Ibby will please give Miss Kephart my regrets."

Isabella nodded wordlessly. Before anyone else could speak, Lowry's little brother Johnny burst out, "Let them all go, Father!" His cheeks flamed with excitement. Lowry managed a smile as the black-haired boy sat bolt upright to appear taller. He was eleven now, and no bigger than Lowry had been at that age, ten years before. "I'm old enough to take the refugees!"

Mother said, "Why, how very kind of you to offer, Johnny. How unselfish!" she declared. "Only—" she paused "—I believe Mr. McCague is expecting you to chop wood these next few days. You know how he depends on you come hog butchering time, in November," she added tactfully. "He needs a hard worker like you to keep his kettles boiling, but that takes a powerful lot of wood."

Johnny's face fell. Then he brightened. "Yes, that's true. Perhaps I can help with a fugitive soon, though, before they have all run away. I would be ever so careful and brave."

Father sighed at his son's flushed, excited face. "Johnny, you are a good lad. I feel sure your turn will come. Yes, and I have no doubt that even little Tappan there—" he gestured to the happy toddler sitting on Mother's lap "—will take his turn on the Underground Road many a time. To all who come, we will give aid," Father finished sadly.

The rest of the family gaped in consternation at the small boy. Ten more years at least must pass before baby Tappan would be old enough to help a refugee. Many pairs of shoulders drooped as the weary years stretched before them. Strangely, Lowry's heart felt much lighter. He was glad that he could help now, for surely the slaves' lot was worse than his own.

With only a twinge of regret, he watched Ibby, David, Calvin, and Samuel settle in the carriage the next morning. They laughed and chattered as they tucked a dust robe over their laps.

"Good-bye, Lowry. Thank you for staying behind. I will be sure to give your message to Miss Kephart," Ibby assured him. Her cheeks were flushed with excitement.

Lowry mustered a grin. "Thanks, Ibby. Please give my kind regards to Mr. Humphries, as well," he added with a touch of impishness.

"Oh! Why, I—I will," his sister faltered as David drove them away. The rest of the family laughed heartily. Everyone knew that Ibby and J. W. Humphries were sweet on each other.

Toward afternoon, a fugitive labored through the trees to the top of the Eminence, footsore, furtive, and hungry. Lowry fed the dispirited soul well and showed him a bed where he could rest safely until dark. Then he went to the barn and saddled two horses. At early candlelight, he and the refugee vanished like smoke into the woods. Lowry led the other horse, because the shattered man threatened to bolt. He was sure his master lay in wait behind every tree.

The rigorous trail traversed the hills and ravines along Red Oak Creek, meandering northeast along a bifurcating stream to the Red Oak settlement. The rain held off, and five and a half clandestine miles of glances darted over the shoulder brought the two to the home of the McCoy brothers, William and James. The doorway stood open, and Lowry stopped the horses just outside a semicircle of glowing lantern light. He walked alone to the door and called. After he had greeted the McCoys, the arrangements fell into place with ease.

"Certainly, Lowry! As a matter of fact, we had just decided to go on to Sardinia tonight instead of tomorrow. It is not so far for us, but we will be better rested in the morning if we leave right away, isn't that right, William?" bubbled Rosanna McCoy, winking at her brother, who merely nodded.

"Rosie, I was thinking along the same lines," exclaimed her twin sister, Rebecca. She parted her coppery hair and swiftly braided, coiled, and pinned it up. As usual, the taciturn brothers offered neither yea nor nay, but cheerfully complied with their loquacious sisters' bidding, to Lowry's amusement. Thank goodness Amanda did not talk so much! He had to admit, though, that the McCoy twins had good hearts.

He turned the fugitive over to their capable care with a word of thanks and swung up on the horse about to leave, but a Rankin never left the McCoy home empty-handed. This time Rosie and Becky thrust into Lowry's hand a steaming apple tart, carefully wrapped in a checkered napkin. With a quick handshake for the burly brothers, and a nod to the vivacious twins, Lowry was off, and another fugitive was safely on the way to Canada. As the sisters waved good-bye, Rosie could not help calling, "See you at the convention!" Lowry gave a sad shake of his head and felt that everyone was having fun but him.

The next day a slant of lemony afternoon sunlight washed the bluff in heavy hazy gold. Lowry whistled in the fenced yard as he chopped wood. He swatted at a cloud of pesky gnats and tried not to think about Sardinia and eyes bluer than a September sky.

A stone rattled down a deep gully on the hillside. Lowry looked up to see Jake Todd approaching with a refugee in tow. The runaway's face glistened with sweat from the sweltering heat of the day. Lowry noticed that the man had a blackened left eye and walked as if he ached. He breathed hard, but not from exertion.

"You alone, Rankin?" greeted Todd.

"Yes, I am, Mr. Todd," Lowry answered slowly.

"Well, I brung you a runaway. Found him hiding in my barn. 'Pears like you Rankins ain't the only ones in Ripley as can help out the poor slave, now, are you?" Todd drawled proudly. His pointy face and glittering eyes roamed the yard as he talked.

Lowry thought fast. He had never known Jake Todd to sympathize with the plight of slaves. In fact, nobody knew on which side of the fence Todd's loyalties lay. Fearing a trap, Lowry decided the less said, the better.

"Thanks, Mr. Todd. Good day," he nodded.

"What are you going to do now, Rankin? It's the middle of the day," reminded Todd. He studied Lowry like a poker hand.

Lowry merely motioned to the refugee. In misery, the man followed Lowry reluctantly into the house and peered one-sidedly about with his good eye.

"You gonna take that *boy* in your house in broad daylight?" Todd called.

Lowry did not answer. He left Todd alone in the yard and watched from behind a curtain until he was sure he had gone. Satisfied, he quickly gave the runaway a drink of water. They left the house by the back door, cutting through the trees to a straw rick near the barn.

"In there," Lowry directed. In mute appeal, the man searched Lowry's face. Lowry stood by the thatched rick as the man dug well in, safely hidden from probing eyes. Then he headed for Ripley.

In every doorway in town, it seemed, a gaggle of men, women, or children gossiped and chatted. Idly, Lowry strolled down the street to the general store and listened.

"My dear, the *dress* she wore!" A lady giggled just inside a parlor window.

"Why, this ol' coonhound of mine can run all night if he's of a mind to!" boasted a man outside a tavern. He rested his hand fondly upon a big dog's speckled head. Ears flopped and tongue lolled as the hound grinned up at his master.

"Ma, we saw him, didn't we?" a boy piped shrilly. "We saw the man they're looking for!" The boy's mother bent to shush him as she dragged him unceremoniously by the hand.

Lowry did not even break stride. He rounded the corner, then stopped short.

"We've got old Uncle Johnny this time!" a man crowed.

A crowd of men, each with pistols securely belted, gestured and spoke in low tones. A short, stocky man stood in the center of the group, slouch hat tipped forward. As he spoke, his wispy moustache, the color of a new copper kettle, fluttered ridiculously. A bitter grin twisted his mouth and his pale olive eyes stared dead and cold. Lowry ducked aside and walked quickly past. Nearby, a passel of horses—roans, whites, paints, bays, sorrels, chestnuts, and blacks—stamped and snuffled along the hitching rail, where they were firmly tied. Lowry noticed bullwhips, handcuffs, and ropes, the tools of the slave catching trade, lashed to the horses' saddles with rawhide thongs. If the fugitive he harbored belonged to this man, he had not a moment to lose. He hurried along to consult with the one person he knew always had her finger on the town's pulse.

Moments later, he stood on the McCagues' wide front porch. Aunt Kittie greeted him and pulled him quickly inside. One look at his tense face told her volumes.

"Mr. McCague just stepped out. That Alice Pratt started all the trouble," Aunt Kittie fumed. "She does not curb Willie as she should. That child would not hush until he had told his news to all the ladies and all the men in the general vicinity, just like he was sharing the gospel. He and his ma saw a fugitive in the woods just below town. Well, who should be passing by but Laban Biggerman?" She pursed her lips primly. "Directly he had garnered up a big body of men just by saying his slave is worth one thousand five hundred dollars." She drew off her gloves finger by finger, slapping them against her palm to emphasize her words.

"Laban Biggerman? Is he that short, red-haired man?" Lowry asked. "Who is he?"

"Adam Lowry," she began, for Aunt Kittie always used both given names, "my child, take especial care, because Biggerman is Tice James's new slave hunter. Biggerman's a hard one, a slave-trader, too, meaner'n a snake. He will post a guard tonight on every road leading out of town. The slave hunters have orders to stop anyone leading an extra horse. The man who tries that shall be subjected to an awful grilling, make no mistake. I fear the questioning will be done none too gently," she cautioned, "for they are nothing but boastful bullies. They will bait you and goad you, calling you and your family abusive names until you can stand no more, hoping you will fight them," she reflected. "They are legion, and there is but one of you." She took his hand. "I will pray for your safety. God go with you." She opened the door, but cried, "Wait!" and hurried into the back room. "I hope you will not have occasion to use these, but if you should meet Biggerman, he may hesitate a bit if he sees you are armed." She slid open a small drawer in her writing desk. She drew out a shining pair of pistols and placed them in his hands. "Now, hurry!" she urged.

Lowry secured the guns. He gazed speculatively at Aunt Kittie in her striped poplin gown and beribboned cap. Beneath the flounce and fluff beat a heart filled with splendid courage and mercy. She looked as if she would like to tear into Laban Biggerman barehanded, but he knew that the instant he left, she would kneel at her bedside to pray for Lowry's safe passage instead. Most likely, she would also pray for the slave hunter's deliverance, he thought wryly, just to heap coals of fire upon his head. Impulsively, he kissed her cheek.

Aunt Kittie cupped her hand to her face in surprise, and then smiled gently. "God love you, Adam Lowry! Good-bye."

As Lowry left the porch, he heard a horse clip-clop away from town along the river. He recognized the rider with disbelief. Lowry glanced back to the McCagues' house, longing to tell Aunt Kittie that one of her prayers had already been answered. Going alone to the next station with a valuable man did not appeal to Lowry; now it seemed that not everyone had gone to the convention, after all. He raised his voice. "Alex! Alex Cunningham!"

The fair-haired, freckled rider drew rein, spotted Lowry, and swung his horse about. The spirited horse soon champed and fretted in front of Lowry, his rider hard pressed to stay seated. From the corner of his eye, Lowry saw one of Biggerman's henchmen eyeing him with a bit too much interest.

"What is it, cousin? You look as though you lost your best friend. Why aren't you in Sardinia tonight?" Alex asked, grinning.

Lowry frowned. With studied carelessness, he said, "Oh, my girl went back on me and went with another fellow."

Alex's eyes nearly popped out of his head. Clearly, he did not believe that Amanda Kephart would choose to go anywhere with anyone but Lowry. Lowry blushed at the lie; if only the eavesdropper swallowed it, though. Uninterested in affairs of the heart, the man sidled away.

Lowry wasted no time. "I need your help," he hissed. "Can I count on you?" All business now, Cunningham agreed with a nod and Lowry set up a time to meet.

At twilight, lanky Alex rode into the Rankins' yard as Lowry hefted a woman's sidesaddle onto Old Sorrel's wide back. Lowry rescued the slave from the straw pile and the two cousins quickly brushed the straw from the man's hair and clothes. The hapless fugitive sneezed once, but otherwise he made no sound at all, his suspicious gaze shifting between Lowry and Alex.

Inside, at the table, Lowry served the runaway a trencher of ham and boiled turnips, heaped with plenty of corn cake. The man drained a tin cup of water but picked at the food listlessly. He answered Lowry's questions with the greatest reluctance. He seemed to believe that he had been delivered into the hands of slave catchers who would return him to Biggerman for the sake of a reward.

"What's your name?" Lowry asked.

"Paul, sir," the slave answered. His jaw muscles twitched.

"Who is your master, Paul?"

They waited for his answer, but he only shook his head, unwilling to meet their eyes. "Come now, I must know who we are up against," Lowry reasoned, but it was like pulling teeth to get anything from the man. "Are you Tice's Paul?"

The abruptness startled the answer from the man. He nodded.

Alex expelled his breath in a noisy rush, but Lowry remained silent. Thunder muttered sullenly in the distance. Lowry watched the man's temple thrum to his rapid pulse. He sat with arms outstretched before him on the table, muscles taut. Something in his attitude made Lowry wonder if this man was a decoy, set to trap his family into revealing their clandestine work. He must find out. Quietly he remarked, "Biggerman is in town."

Paul exploded toward the door like a fox before hounds. The chair clattered to the puncheon floor with a fearful racket. Lowry and Alex lunged for the runaway as he bolted. They seized him and dragged him back to the table as he struggled vainly between the two of them.

Satisfied that the man truly desired to go to Canada, Lowry commented, "Good. Now listen to me. We are your friends. If you stay with us, you will be safe, but if you do not, you will be caught, for Biggerman has posted a watch on every road. If you follow orders, you will be safely conveyed to Canada, where you will be free."

Paul's chest heaved as he considered their words. A slow change came over his face.

"Now, Paul, you must eat, for we have a hard night's work ahead of us. We still have sufficient time before dark," Lowry reassured kindly. He pushed the food toward him. With freedom in sight, however, Paul refused to taste another morsel.

"Let's go now, sir," he urged. "I'm ready." He bore no resemblance to the desperate slave of five minutes ago. He held his head high.

Lowry looked ruefully at Alex—another missed meal. They heard a commotion in the front room as Mother and Father returned from town, younger children in tow. Lowry raced to block the fugitive from view and shook his head slightly at his parents. Without batting an eyelash, Mother quickly ushered the children upstairs. She knew that the fewer people who knew about Paul, the better.

Father came to the table. He noted the runaway's puffed eye and hunched posture. His face grew red with indignation as he saw that the talk in town was true. He faced the man and vowed through gritted teeth, "Though he should follow you to Canada,

Laban Biggerman shall never again lay so much as one finger on you." At these forceful words, Paul's stony eyes softened.

However, a shadow crossed his face and trouble returned to the slave's voice. "Sir, he said that if he needed to, he could find me anywhere I go. He said . . ." but here Paul hesitated.

"Suppose you tell us what he said," Father prompted calmly.

"He said, 'Even if y'all was to go to hell, make no mistake, I'll find you.'"

Father smiled a wry smile and his eyes danced in amusement. "You had better avoid that place, Paul. You will be more likely to meet him there than anywhere else."

The slave hesitated a moment. "I believe you mean that, sir," he said, wonder in his voice. A fleeting smile crossed his lips.

Aware of the passing time, Lowry and Alex tersely outlined their plans. In the gathering dusk they escorted the slave to the barn where the horses waited. Paul noted the sidesaddle on his horse and hung back. Lowry explained, "I thought perhaps they might not question me so closely when I return if they think the horse is for a lady." Satisfied, Paul mounted, and he, Lowry, and Alex started their journey.

Cautiously they led the horses into the timber, where the rising wind swirled and lifted the leaves, revealing their pale undersides. Intermittent sheet lightning flashed in the steely gray clouds overhead. Dry cornstalks rustled as the boys entered the dense shelter of Father's cornfield opposite the barn.

They had gone no more than a few rods when suddenly Lowry stopped and held up his hand. As the wind blew toward them out of the west, he imagined he heard a faint murmur. Straining his ears, he caught the sound again, a sibilant hiss, then an answering hum. There was no mistake. He heard voices. Had Laban Biggerman's siege already begun?

Chapter 13

LOWRY SET OUT TO FIND THE speakers' whereabouts. He scanned the cornfield. A craggy white oak stood outlined in the center of the field against the growing darkness, the jagged dead limbs scratching the sky. Lowry angled with the wind at his back to carry the noise of their passing away from the other sounds. When they reached the dead tree, he motioned for Alex and Paul to stay there beneath its shelter. He handed his horse's bridle to Alex and crept along the edge of the cornfield, ears honed for the murmurs, which were much more distinct now. Still downwind, he stealthily parted the cornstalks and peered out.

Four dark shapes crouched at the edge of the potato patch—no, five! Biggerman himself knelt among the men; Lowry recognized the slaveholder's slouch hat, dimly visible in the fading light. Heads close together, the men watched the road leading west away from the back of the house, down the hill to town. Lowry and his friends had barely escaped detection.

Lowry followed the cornrow and cut through the woods to the east of the house, planning all the way. He entered the front door and startled his family considerably. He quickly informed his father of the situation.

"Let's give them something to watch, Father," Lowry said with a grim smile.

Father's eyes flashed as he and Mother listened and nodded at Lowry's plan. They sprang into action. Lowry noticed Johnny and Andrew watching wistfully. He beckoned them as Mother readied two lanterns.

"Can you fellows help me? Will you be very brave and do all I say?" Lowry solemnly questioned.

Faces on fire with determination, the two nodded their dark heads.

"That's capital! Now, Biggerman and his men are watching the house. I want them to see you go out to the barn with your lanterns. Walk slowly. Stop now and then. Raise your lanterns to see in the shadows or turn around and put them down. When you get to the barn, saddle a horse or do whatever you think will keep those cowards watching until we can get well away. Do not be afraid," he encouraged, but he needn't have worried. His little brothers' eyes gleamed with mischief. "Father will come and get you when the men have gone," Lowry concluded.

Mother handed a lantern to Andrew and pressed her cheek to his. Father smiled at his namesake.

"Well, Johnny, so you are helping a refugee at last!" he congratulated as he gave him the other lantern.

Johnny looked at his father with wordless adoration. More than any of his brothers, Lowry knew this one wanted nothing more than to be just like Father.

"All ready?" he asked, and the two proud boys bobbed jauntily through the back door, lanterns swinging in the darkness. Lowry watched them go and bade the rest of the family goodbye again. Stealthily he slunk toward the landmark of the lone oak. Thunder growled, closer this time. The night grew very black as the wind chattered through the cornstalks. Lowry felt his way through the uneven rows, correcting his course now and then with the oak tree's darker silhouette.

Alex looked up anxiously as he heard Lowry approach. Lowry indicated that they should lead the horses to the northeast. The other two followed him closely, Indian file, to the opposite corner of the field, where Lowry quickly let down the rails of Father's fence. Heads down, the horses carefully picked their way across the lowered bars. On the other side, Lowry swung the bars back up and slid them into place. He gave Paul a leg up on Old Sorrel's broad back. Paul sat further back in the saddle than he was accustomed to avoid the lady's leg rest and his right foot dangled with no stirrup to rest on. They rode horseback for the first time, quartering through Father's wood lot.

As Lowry led the way down a deep ravine, he leaned back in the saddle to spare his horse's back on the steep descent. Paul and Alex followed suit, each with an arm upraised to shield their faces from the thin, whippy branches that snapped back at them. In only a few minutes, they reached the bottomland and leaned forward as the stalwart horses labored up the other side. Paul patted Old Sorrel's satiny neck and the friendly gelding tossed his head and slogged forward.

As they gained the top of a ridge, another of Father's endless cornfields greeted them. Silent heat lightning shot like quicksilver across the floor of the clouds. Lowry headed northeast at an angle across the field. He pushed on as quickly as safety permitted. Soon his ears picked up the welcome gurgle of Red Oak Creek, concealed for miles by thick timber. He led the way into the tangled brush, then slightly downhill. Halfway down to the creek he stopped, then signaled Alex, followed by Paul, to take the lead along the hillside, keeping the creek well below them, the ridge well above. Biggerman's posse might scout the ridge, the creek, or both, but no one would think to check halfway down the hill. Instinctively the riders leaned to the uphill side, distributing their weight as evenly as possible. Lowry noted gratefully that the wind and thunder masked the sound of their passage.

Gradually the heat lightning subsided. The night grew as sooty black as a crow's wing. Even with the horses traveling practically nose to tail, Lowry could not see the two men ahead of him.

"Alex!" he whispered.

"Yes?"

"Call out quietly now and then. I cannot see even two inches before my eyes. We must stay together. Paul?"

"Here, sir," Paul answered briefly, and the three continued, whispering at intervals as the long ride continued.

"Lowry!" Alex hissed. "I think we may have come to the road. How do we cross?" How, indeed, Lowry wondered. A long, bare ridge separated the woods from the public road. If they crossed it, they would be in plain sight whenever lightning flashed.

A white flash lit their startled faces and a mighty rumble of thunder rolled across the hillside. Old Sorrel spooked and swerved, and his ghostly tail fanned in the wind. A few icy raindrops pattered down the wind and spurted into the dust with muddy splashes the size of silver cartwheels. Ranks of trees bowed low as a cold blast of wind elbowed through. The little band hunched their shoulders in resignation as the rain cascaded. The deluge blotted everything from sight.

With a rueful grin, Lowry answered Alex's question. "Here's how we cross the road, Alex. In the rain," he gibed, and the three chuckled in spite of themselves. Sopping wet and chilled to the bone, the other two blindly followed Lowry. The one consolation was that Biggerman's gang would fare no better. Cheered somewhat, the young men set out across the open field, their horses skidding in soupy mud.

If the horses' hooves made any sound as they crossed the road, no one heard it over the roar of the cataract through which they passed. If Biggerman's men lay nearby, it made not a particle of difference. Alex, Paul, and Lowry passed unseen through the gray curtain.

Hour after hour for twenty long miles, the horses slogged through the pouring rain. Though Lowry shifted position to keep his drenched clothes away from his skin, it did no good, he discovered. Water streamed down his neck from his drenched hat brim. The honest smell of steamy horseflesh mingled with the scent of waterlogged saddle leather as the horses staggered and pulled their hooves from cuppy mud laden with heavy clay. About an hour before daylight, the rain tapered to a fine mist, and the three riders shivered into the Reverend John Mahan's yard.

On the front porch, Lowry and Alex parted company with Paul. Never again would anyone call him Tice's Paul. He belonged only to himself now.

"I'm sorry I tried to run from y'all," he apologized, ashamed. "No one's ever done for me before what you boys done."

"God be with you, Paul," Lowry replied.

Paul smiled and followed Reverend Mahan's wife into the house.

Lowry turned to Reverend Mahan, all business despite aching tiredness. "May we curry our horses and clean their hooves? They are about done in, but we can make them more comfortable." Reverend Mahan hurried to the barn while Alex and Lowry unsaddled their mounts. With the borrowed currycombs, they scoured the caked runnels of mud from the horses' bellies and legs as they talked.

"Sir, that man belonged to Tice James," Lowry began as he worked. "He's not much of a threat, but his new slave hunter is. Name's Biggerman." Briefly, he detailed the lengths to which Biggerman had already gone to recapture Paul. As he finished, he emphasized, "Reverend Mahan, it is not safe to keep him here. You will see that he is moved on right away, I trust." Lowry glanced up at the minister as if certain of his answer. Then he returned to cleaning the balled mud from Old Sorrel's right front hoof and quickly rubbed down the tired legs. The orangey-brown horse stretched his upper lip in ecstasy at the attention, then curved his neck around to bump Lowry with his nose, nickering.

"Don't you worry, Lowry. I will see that he is well taken care of. You just come in and have a bite of breakfast. You must be done in," the minister sidestepped.

Something about the man's casual tone alarmed Lowry. "You will see that Paul gets safely away immediately, Reverend Mahan? It is very dangerous for you to keep him here. Dangerous for him, and for you," Lowry pressed.

"Now, Lowry, you folks in Ripley have your way of doing things, and we here in Sardinia have ours. We will see that Paul is safe," Reverend Mahan cajoled.

"Reverend Mahan, surely you believe that it is best to keep the fugitive ahead of the pursuers?" Lowry questioned with some asperity.

"Well, that is the opinion of some of my neighbors, but I feel that to keep him about here a few days would disarm suspicion, just as though he belonged here. After all," Reverend Mahan chided, "Ohio is a free state, Lowry."

Once he would have agreed, but he was immeasurably wiser now. He stifled his anger and replied evenly, "But Laban Biggerman is from Kentucky."

Reverend Mahan peered doubtfully through the shadows at Lowry's stony face, then thrust out his own bottom lip obstinately.

Alex spoke up. "Well, Lowry, we'd best be going on to the convention."

Lowry checked an angry retort. Swiftly, the cousins saddled the horses. Lowry made an extraordinary effort to be pleasant. "Good day, Reverend Mahan. I hope you'll move Paul on immediately, for your own safety as well as his. It is as much as his life is worth to keep him here for Biggerman to find."

Reverend Mahan drew himself up stubbornly, replying only, "Good day, Lowry."

Lowry shook his head and spurred his horse. The thought that their hard ride in the rain might come to naught brought home the seeming futility of moving hundreds of slaves north, one man at a time. Lowry led Old Sorrel and the remaining miles passed without incident. In the early morning, the mist subsided.

Soon they reached the convention grounds, just outside Sardinia. Sunday morning services were over, and scores of young people milled about as they prepared for the long drive home.

"Lowry, suppose someone is here for Biggerman? Won't he see you leading Old Sorrel . . ." Alex worried in a low voice.

Lowry did not reply. Instead, he eagerly searched the crowd in the grove and caught a glimpse of golden curls. "Thank you for your help, Alex! Best if we separate now. Will you excuse me, please?" He ignored Alex's astounded expression.

"Mandy! Wait for me," Lowry called.

Amanda Kephart whirled, her face surprised and happy.

"Why, Lowry!" she exclaimed.

"May I speak with you for a moment?" he asked nonchalantly.

"Of course! My, it's good to see you again," she began, but he interrupted and explained in a rapid undertone how he came to be there.

"So, will you allow me to escort you home? You may ride Old Sorrel, if you wish," he offered.

"I'd like that, Lowry. Thank you." She rejoined her group and said something that made them laugh. With a wave of her hand, she came back to Lowry and handed him her bundle of going-away clothing, neatly done up in an apron. He looped it over the pommel and held Old Sorrel as she prepared to mount.

A grinning Alex trotted past the couple as Lowry helped Amanda climb the upping block. "Well, well, well, it appears Lowry Rankin brought a horse twenty-one miles just for a special young lady to ride! Is she ready to kiss and make up, cousin?" he teased, loud enough for the young people around him to hear. In amusement, the other fellows took up the taunt as the girls giggled. Alex laughed at Lowry's consternation and urged his horse along with a cheerful wave.

"Never mind, Lowry," Amanda consoled. "I understand." She smiled encouragingly.

The memory of the miserable ride in the rain faded, and for the first time since last Thursday, Lowry relaxed. "Don't mind my cousin," he answered quietly. "He meant to help my case. I could wish, perhaps, that he had chosen another method, but the fact is," Lowry bowed gallantly, "I *did* bring this horse especially for you," he grinned. "He just had some other work to do first," he added, slapping Old Sorrel's neck.

As they started for Ripley, Lowry felt happier than he had in weeks. Amanda sang a song that lilted in a minor key as Old Sorrel strode through a sunny field of black-eyed Susans that powdered his damp legs and broad chest with golden pollen. Still full of go even after his long night in the rain, he seemed proud to bear the girl. She sang a hymn she'd learned at the convention:

> If thou but suffer God to guide thee,
> And hope in Him thru all thy ways,
> He'll give thee strength, what-e'er betide thee,
> And bear thee thru the evil days;
> Who trusts in God's unchanging love
> Builds on the rock that naught can move.

The two horses waltzed in an easy canter and their tails windmilled to the music as the couple rode home to the Eminence. Lowry felt there would never be a better time. He reined in his mount. "Amanda, I—"

"I'll race you to the pike!" Amanda teased. She touched her heels to Old Sorrel's flanks and crouched low over his neck, her face all but buried in the horse's whipping mane. Her sunbonnet twirled like a kite with no tail as wisps of her golden hair straggled. The riding skirt rippled and snapped like a flag. She threw back her head and laughed aloud as Old Sorrel left Lowry's horse in the dust.

Lowry's hair clung to his forehead in rain-damp spikes and his shirt stuck to his back. His horse stood where he had stopped it for a breather, with one back leg knuckled beneath, hip slack. The poor animal's head drooped and he looked as tired as Lowry felt, but he chirruped and coaxed it into a stiff-legged trot that jarred his teeth. He had something important to ask Amanda, and now was the time.

Before he caught up with her, shouts filled the air. A phalanx of horsemen charged headlong down a ridge toward the pike. Lowry counted six men before he recognized Laban Biggerman in the lead on a fiery, red-gold gelding. The slave hunter raked his horse's flanks with his spurs and drew blood, and the sun glittered on gunmetal.

In a flash, the slave hunters had surrounded Amanda. Lowry saw Old Sorrel half-rear and utter a defiant neigh, but Amanda crouched forward and kept her seat. The good-natured horse actually laid back his ears and snapped as Biggerman grabbed for the reins. Then Amanda was a prisoner, just like in Lowry's nightmare.

Before Lowry thought of the danger, he snapped off a long, whippy branch and cut his horse's flank mercilessly until they shouldered roughly to Amanda's side. With his heart in his mouth lest Amanda should unwittingly give him away, he faced Biggerman, the leader. The man's olive eyes were no longer cold and dead. They sparkled with hate.

"Where you been, darlin'?" he drawled. He did not address his impudent question to Amanda. He looked straight at Lowry.

Lowry returned Biggerman's stare. "If you make it your business to know, I've been to the music convention in Sardinia."

"Where's she been, then?" Biggerman jerked his head at Amanda. Lowry opened his mouth to answer, but Biggerman silenced him. "She can answer for herself."

Amanda's voice came clearly from the confines of her sunbonnet, which she had drawn protectively over her head. "I was with him at the convention."

"That's a lie," the slave hunter snarled. "Ain't that right, Clem?"

Lowry looked at the man and his heart sank. Clem was the stranger who had overheard him say that Amanda went with another fellow to the convention. Clem grinned and tipped his hat.

"Think I don't know who you are, boy, and what you're always up to?" Biggerman sneered. "You're Lowry Rankin, and this here's Amanda Kephart, your gal. Your pa's Uncle Johnny Rankin, who steals slaves. You brought Tice's Paul to Sardinia last night. That about reckon it all up square?" He spat. "I make it my business to know all about them that crosses me and Mr. James."

Lowry thought fast. Did Biggerman actually believe what he had said? Lowry wanted to deny what Biggerman had accused him of, but he decided to call his bluff instead. He set his jaw and said nothing as he stared at the slave hunter.

The stillness stretched. A goldfinch skipped down a stray breeze, and Old Sorrel jerked his head in surprise.

Biggerman broke his gaze. "Come on, boys! We don't need a puny preacher boy to tell us what's what. We got us a slave to catch!" He whistled, and the slave hunters whipped up their horses. Then they were gone.

"I pray that Mahan moved Paul on last night. Oh, Amanda!" Lowry let out a long breath. "Are you all right?"

She faced him. He had never seen her eyes so big. "How did you know what to do?" she whispered.

"I did just what I always do." He hung his head. "Nothing."

"You call that nothing? Why, you saved us!" Amanda pushed back her sunbonnet and held out her hand. "See? I'm shaking yet! I was never so frightened in my life!"

He pointed to a fallen tree near the pike. "Let's rest." Gently he helped her dismount and spread his handkerchief over the wet bark. She smoothed her skirt and sat down. Lowry joined her under the shade of a smooth-barked beech tree, but it was only a bit less muggy there. The morning sun shone hot, and mist from yesterday's rain steamed up from the ground as the horses grazed a little way off. Somewhere nearby, a rain-swollen creek hurled itself over broken rocks.

Lowry stared up at the beech leaves that rustled overhead. When the slave hunters and Biggerman had surrounded Amanda, a thousand lifetimes had passed before his eyes. For one terror-stricken moment, he had experienced what Mrs. Stowe had witnessed at the slave auction, separation from the one he loved most. He shuddered. If Amanda had been black instead of white, Biggerman could have stolen her from him, and he would have been helpless to prevent it. He would have lost her forever.

"Mandy, I need to ask you something." Desperation made him talk fast. At her quizzical look, he took her hand. "I never would have chosen this time to speak of it. I certainly would not have chosen this place. If it had been my choice, I would have taken you walking in our peach orchard in the springtime, when the white peach blossoms shower down on the wind."

She blushed furiously and looked away. She picked at a speck of lint on her sleeve and made several unfruitful attempts to brush it away.

"I don't have a job—since I've left Lane, I don't even have the prospect of one. But Mandy, I love you. When I knew it at last, I was so afraid I would lose you! Marry me, Amanda. I have nothing to offer you but my love. I have failed at everything I ever tried, but I promise to work hard, if only you will accept." He could hardly breathe.

"Tell me how you've failed, Lowry."

So she was going to make him own up to it. He took a deep breath and confessed as much as he dared to risk. He told her about Sherwood's abduction and escape, his unwitting role in the escape of Tice's David, and his failure as a carpenter. He told her about the slave girl he could not save, the constant persecution from the pro-slavery people in Cincinnati, and the potatoes, saltwater, and brooms. He told her about the endless interruptions to his studies caused by his hundred or so trips to transport slaves, his involuntary revelations while he was feverish, and the Stowe's insistence that he leave his studies to save his health.

"Now I can't be an abolition minister. I've lost too much time. I have to make something of myself, I realize, before I am deserving of you. I need to *do* something with my life," he finished.

"How I envy you, Lowry." Amanda said the words quietly, like a prayer.

He sought her face in bewilderment. "Mrs. Stowe used the same word, *envy*. What do you mean? I am nothing but a miserable failure!"

"Lowry, listen to me." She took his hand. "Don't you see how God has used you? He uses you almost every day, trusts you with the least of His brethren. Think of the hope you give to the slaves who see your light from the other side of the river. Think of the difference you made in their lives because you did what God wanted, and not what you wanted."

For the first time in a long while, Lowry felt a thrill of hope in his heart, but Amanda was not finished. Her eyes were twin stars.

"I think I loved you that day in the schoolyard, when you walked in with your father. But now, well, it's more than that. There is no one I respect more. There is no one I would rather share my life with, no matter what the circumstances." She smiled. "'Better is little with the fear of the Lord than great treasure and trouble therewith.' I love you, Lowry. Yes, I will marry you."

The world did not seem large enough to contain his happiness. He laughed aloud for joy, and Amanda laughed with him, a soft, tremulous laugh. He stood and helped her to her feet. She turned her face to his and he bent to claim a kiss at last, to seal the engagement. Then he sobered. Her welfare was his responsibility now.

"There are so many things I don't know. Maybe—maybe I'll go back to Lane. I have no money, and we may have to live with my folks for a while. And there will always be more refugees from across the river who need my help. It is a difficult life. I don't know how we'll manage, Mandy."

Her eyes softened. "But I know how, Lowry. We'll manage *together*."